IMAAN

Manoranjan Byapari was born in the mid-fifties in Barishal, former East Pakistan. His family migrated to West Bengal in India when he was three. They were resettled in Bankura at the Shiromanipur Refugee Camp. Later, they were forced to shift to the Gholadoltala Refugee Camp, 24-Parganas, and lived there till 1969. However, Byapari had to leave home at the age of fourteen to do odd jobs. In his early twenties, he came into contact with the Naxals and with the famous labour activist Shankar Guha Niyogi. Byapari was sent to jail during this time, where he taught himself to read and write. Later, while working as a rickshaw-puller in Kolkata, Byapari had a chance meeting with the renowned Bengali writer Mahasweta Devi, who urged him to write for her journal *Bartika*. He has written twenty-seven books since. Some of his important works include *Chhera Chhera Jibon*, *Ittibrite Chandal Jibon* (memoir), the *Chandal Jibon Trilogy* (novels) and *Motua Ek Mukti Senar Naam*. Until 2018, he was working as a cook at the Hellen Keller Institute for the Deaf and Blind in West Bengal.

In 2018, the English translation of Byapari's memoir, *Ittibrite Chandal Jibon* (*Interrogating My Chandal Life*), received the Hindu Prize for non-fiction. In 2019, he was awarded the Gateway Lit Fest Writer of the Year Prize. Also, the English translation of his novel *Batashe Baruder Gandha* (*There's Gunpowder in the Air*) was shortlisted for the JCB Prize for Literature 2019, the DSC Prize for South Asian Literature 2019, the Crossword Book Award for Best Translation 2019 and the Mathrubhumi Book of the Year Prize 2020. He was appointed chairman of the newly instituted Dalit Sahitya Akademi in Bengal in 2020.

In 2021, Byapari was elected a member to the Bengal Legislative Assembly as a Trinamool Congress candidate.

Arunava Sinha translates classic, modern and contemporary Bengali fiction and non-fiction into English. Seventy-one of his translations have been published so far. Twice the winner of the Crossword translation award, for Sankar's *Chowringhee* (2007) and Anita Agnihotri's *Seventeen* (2011), respectively, and the winner of the Muse India translation award (2013) for Buddhadeva Bose's *When the Time is Right*, he has also been shortlisted for the Independent Foreign Fiction Prize (2009) for his translation of *Chowringhee* and for the Global Literature in Libraries Initiative Translated YA Book Prize for his translation of Md Zafar Iqbal's *Rasha*, and longlisted for the Best Translated Book Award, USA, 2018 for his translation of Bhaskar Chakravarti's *Things That Happen and Other Poems*. In 2021, his translation of Taslima Nasrin's *Shameless* was shortlisted for the National Translation Award in the USA. Besides India, his translations have been published in the UK and the US in English, and in several European and Asian countries through further translation.

Currently, he is an associate professor of practice in the Creative Writing department at Ashoka University, and Co-Director, Ashoka Centre for Translation.

MANORANJAN BYAPARI

IMAAN

Translated from the Bengali
by Arunava Sinha

eka

eka

First published in Bengali as *Chhera Chhera Jibon* in 2019 by Eka, an imprint of Westland Publications Private Limited

Published in English as *Imaan* in 2021 by Eka, an imprint of Westland Publications Private Limited

Published in English as *Imaan* in 2022 by Eka, an imprint of Westland Books, a division of Nasadiya Technologies Private Limited

No. 269/2B, First Floor, 'Irai Arul', Vimalraj Street, Nethaji Nagar, Allappakkam Main Road, Maduravoyal, Chennai 600095

Westland and the Westland logo are the trademarks of Nasadiya Technologies Private Limited, or its affiliates.

ISBN: 9789395073530

10 9 8 7 6 5 4 3 2 1

Typeset by Jojy Philip, New Delhi 110 015
Printed at Manipal Technologies Limited, Manipal

1

A deafening cry rang out in the confined air this side of the sky-high wall, signifying a name, a distressed existence, the social identity of an individual. From east to west it drifted, and then to the south, before returning to the east.

Whatever the dictionary meaning of the word Imaan might be, in this case, it was the name of an eighteen-year-old young man. Who was a prisoner. It was him that the raaitar was calling out for in a dreadful tone. I-m-a-a-n Aliiiiiiii.

Sitting in a corner of the juvenile ward, the chhokra file, as it was called there, Imaan had heard the cry but was unmoved, pretending he had not heard it. For it was beyond his comprehension that it was his name, that someone could be actually calling for him by his name. Not once in these eighteen long years had anyone called him by his name for any reason whatsoever. And with time, the very faith that someone could address him by his name had been eroded. The name had gathered the dust of years of disuse, its layers so thick that Imaan Ali was unable to blow them away and seek his own identity beneath them.

It was a long time ago when, trembling with delight at hearing his name being announced by the raaitar Shekhar Roy, he had thrown away the boiled peas served for breakfast and raced towards the kestebil, where prisoners' files were handled. Counting off his age on his fingers, he had calculated that he was sixteen years and seven months old. He had felt hope: he would be released from imprisonment now, and he would take his place in the world of free people that he could see through the window of his ward. All the conditions for his release had been met, which was why the raaitar was calling for him. Before the joy of freedom in his heart, his meal of worm-infested peas had seemed worthless. His friend Cartoon, an inmate of the same ward, had said, 'Quick, the raaitar's calling for you! Looks like your ship's ready to sail.'

But Imaan's hopes were dashed when the guard's baton came down on his back.

'*Kaiko tu aaya idhar?* Who called you, what did you come here for?'

Here, the stick spoke before words could. Along with the blow from his baton, Bapuram, the prison guard, had roared, 'Fuck off! You'll never be released. You'll die in jail.'

'What happened?' Cartoon had asked.

'It wasn't for me,' Imaan had said, rubbing his shoulder where the baton had landed. 'Some other Imaan.' His eyes had flooded with tears. 'I'll never be free. This jail is where I'll live and where I'll die.'

Which was why Imaan felt today that it wasn't him but someone else whom they were calling for. There was no count of how many of the three thousand or four thousand prisoners here might be named Imaan. It must be one of them. ...

It was late in the afternoon. All the gates leading into the wards had been opened, giving the inmates a chance to take a stroll in the yard outside, which was fenced in with iron railings. They would be allowed a couple of hours here to get some fresh air and sunlight, before being given their dinner and sent back behind the strong metal gates by six in the evening. Then the entire evening and night would pass locked inside the heat and humidity of the ward. The brass locks would be opened again at six in the morning, followed by another two hours outside, including the morning meal. Boiled peas or chickpeas, flattened rice with jaggery, muri ... a different item every day. Sometimes a thin gruel too.

Imaan hadn't been outside today because he was feeling out of sorts. It seemed like he had a fever coming on. He was lying down, waiting for the crowds to thin before going out to collect his dinner. Imaan didn't want to go to the hospital for such an everyday illness. And what use would it be anyway, since just two medicines were available there—a red liquid in a bottle and white tablets. Any cuts or bruises or contusions meant a dab of the red fluid, and everything from malaria or TB to typhoid or simple fever meant white pills three times a day.

At that moment, the thundering cry pierced his eardrums again. Imaan Aliiiiiii ... But this one was different from the voice that had been reverberating within the enclosed jail compound earlier. There was no mistake, it was his friend Cartoon who was shouting out his name. Soon afterwards, the cry turned into a chorus as all the fellow inmates of the chhokra file sang a collective song of freedom for a prisoner—'Come quick, Imaan. You're going to be released, your papers are here.'

Jail! The harshest and most inhuman word in the world. Shorn of all the rules, regulations and practices of the civilised world, and occupied by heartless, violent, trigger-happy humanoids. All of them are dangerous criminals convicted under various sections of the Indian Penal Code. But then there are some innocent people in jail, too, who have no family or friends outside with the financial muscle to help. The Indian legal system is mighty but expensive—beyond the purchasing power of poor people, who are therefore forced to rot by injustice, without even being tried, in their dark prison cells.

Imaan had had no choice but to spend most of his life so far amongst these criminals, without having committed a crime himself. Ever since he had entered this prison in his mother's arms at the age of six months, he had had no chance to return to the world of free people. No one had stepped up to secure his release. The enormous universe that lay beyond whatever he could see from the window of the ward was unknown, unexplored.

He didn't exactly know what charges had brought his mother Zahura Bibi to jail. By the time he was old enough to understand that, there was no one here who knew the facts of the case—some of those who knew had been released before serving their entire sentence, while others had got free early by dying. But Zahura Bibi's dusty, faded case file must still have been lying somewhere in the jail or in Alipur

Court. It might even have been found if someone were to search for it—but who would look, and why?

There was a particular incident in this jail that was often recounted. A prisoner who had been given a life sentence entered the jail when his daughter was very young. She grew up, studied law, became an advocate, dusted out the old file of her father's case, and went to court asking for a retrial. She fought the new case, had her father exonerated, and secured his release.

But there was no such luck for Zahura Bibi. However, were anyone to stumble on the file, they would learn that a village woman had killed her husband with a blow on the head from a crowbar. The man was involved with many other women, and would come home drunk every night and beat his wife up. One day, she couldn't take it any longer and, picking up whatever was at hand, hit him with it. It turned out to be the crowbar. She was sentenced to ten years in jail. The trial and sentencing hadn't taken long because she had confessed voluntarily.

It was the investigating officer who had given her the advice. 'Look, Zahura Bibi, you did do it after all, so you can't escape punishment, whether heavy or light. But if you confess you did it, the sentence will be shorter. You must tell the magistrate—hujoor, he used to come home drunk every night and beat me up, he had relationships with other women too, I killed him in a rage. The magistrate is a human being too. He can be kind as well. If you cry and tell him the truth, who knows, he might even exonerate you. Or, even if he doesn't do that, he may send you to jail for only a year or two. But if you don't do this, when it's proved you killed your husband—all these people in the village saw you, they'll definitely give evidence—you could be hanged. Think about it, you have a child ... who will look after him if you're hanged?'

Zahura Bibi had walked to the police station with her baby in her arms soon after killing her husband with the crowbar. The police had arrested her at once, but the trial began two years later. She had spent those two years in the female ward in Alipur Jail, without her case coming up in the courts. No one had come to see her. 'You're not part of the family anymore,' Zahura's abbu and amma had told her the day she eloped with Shohidul. 'We don't care whether you live or die, we'll have nothing to do with you, and you'll have nothing to do with us.'

They had kept their word, not bothering to show up even at her darkest hour. As for Shohidul's family, there was obviously no question of their visiting his killer.

Like many others, Shohidul, too, had built a shack on the bed of the dead Vidyadhari river, and fenced off a small patch of land to grow vegetables on it. With his fishing net, he would go to a nearby river or creek, selling his catch to buy rice, daal, salt and oil. Zahura Bibi was hardworking, too, gathering cow dung and turning it into manure to sell to farmers; she had some hens and ducks too. Between their efforts, they survived. In fact, it wouldn't be wrong to say Zahura Bibi was happy.

But, as they say, happiness is not for everyone. Which was exactly what ensued, as joy turned to ashes for Zahura. Shohidul was already addicted to alcohol, but then everyone hereabouts drank to some extent. The women sought comfort by telling one another, 'They're men, after all. They work so hard all day, their bodies start aching. How will they work the next day if they don't drink at night?' Zahura had accepted it too. But what she couldn't accept was the thing Shohidul had for women. Jolil Molla used to live three or four doors away; Shohidul began an affair with his daughter, Najma. And this led to bitter quarrels. Shohidul began to come home drunk and beat up Zahura. Then came that fateful night, when, during a fight, Shohidul uttered the fatal word: talaq. That was it; Zahura Bibi flew into a red-hot rage. Without giving him the chance to pronounce the word the remaining two times, she brought the crowbar down on his head. Shohidul slumped to the floor.

Two years to the trial, and then one year to the verdict. It wasn't a particularly complicated case, after all, since the accused had confessed to killing her husband. Ten years in jail and a fine of two thousand rupees, with an added six months in lieu of the fine.

Zahura Bibi couldn't afford to pay the fine, but she didn't serve ten-and-a-half years either, for she died within three years. She was already suffering from TB, which worsened inside the prison, where medical facilities were not very advanced. The outcome: *kes khallas*.

Imaan was a little child when he entered the jail in his mother's arms. He could be said to be the youngest person on the subcontinent to have been honoured with the status of a prisoner. He was only six-and-a-half when his mother died. Had someone made an application to the judge, stating that they wanted to take complete responsibility for this child, Imaan would not have had to stay in prison. But no such application came, and Imaan remained here.

The first time he was let out of jail, it was to be sent to Mullick Juvenile Home, where young vagrants, unclaimed children and underage criminals were held captive. After spending nearly ten years there, he was sent back to Central Jail at the age of sixteen years and three months. The authorities would now decide whether to keep him jailed or set him free—a right that the administrators of Mullick Juvenile Home did not have. And so, Imaan had spent the past two years in this ward.

There were thirty or forty other boys of Imaan's age here, all of them slapped with cases of some sort. So they were taken to the court every fortnight for their trials. Some were found guilty and sentenced, and the others were set free. Some managed to secure their release on bail. Newcomers took the empty spaces they had left behind. Life was in a state of flux here, ebbing and flowing constantly.

Imaan was not a criminal. He had not been accused of anything, nor sentenced. Since no one came to meet him at the end of the month, the raaitar never called out his name. He wasn't sent to the court either. Like a nameless, unknown weed, he languished in a corner of the prison. Days went by, nights, too, and then months and years. Under pressure of work, the jail authorities forgot he was a human, or that he was here, or why he was here. And so, he never received permission to leave the jail and step into the free world outside.

He had heard that when he turned eighteen years and six months, he would be considered capable of taking responsibility for himself and be released from prison. Imaan didn't know what the world outside was like. Naturally, he was excited about finding out, but along with the anticipation, there was also a trepidation that gnawed away at his heart.

On one occasion, a group of honoured guests were flown to India by the Tourism Department to take a tour of various cities. The idea was that they should go back home and write glowing articles in their newspapers and magazines, leading everyone to believe that India is truly *saare jahan se achha*, so that droves of international tourists would rush to the country. So all the beggars and vagabonds and blind and crippled pavement-dwellers were rounded up and dumped in jail to prevent visual pollution.

After all, what if a filthy, cadaverous beggar were to accost one of the respected guests, while their car was waiting at a traffic signal, and implore them, 'Today no food, give me one rupee, God save you.' This ungrammatical English and horrifying demand would grind the reputation of the country to dust. Hence this preventive measure. The education system in our country is in such a shambles that not even the beggars of posh areas of Calcutta, like Park Street and Chowringhee, had learnt English properly. There are no institutes to provide adequate training. Everything is far more advanced abroad. Those who ask people for money there play the guitar and sing, and are well-dressed; they don't claim they haven't eaten for two days.

But not all of the seventy thousand permanent beggars of Calcutta, not to mention the seasonal beggars and the itinerant beggars, could be caught. Not that the police wanted to capture all of them; all they wanted to do was send out a message that going out on the streets to beg would mean a shortcut to prison. It worked. As soon as a couple of them were forced into a police van, the rest fled the city, some on trains and buses, some on foot. And those who could not leave had to ignore their hunger and retreat into their hovels.

The beggars were released from jail once the visitors had completed their tour of Calcutta. For nearly two months, they had been housed and fed in jail; it was impossible to host them any longer. It would have been another matter had they committed thefts or robberies; for then, the government would have had no choice. But these people were completely innocent.

When their names began to be called out for release, one of the beggars hid in the toilet, refusing to leave. In a stricken voice, he said, 'Bhai, there are maybe three or four thousand thieves and robbers and murderers and rapists in here, at most. But millions outside. Here, at least, you know who they are. But you cannot identify any of them out there. Every single one outside is a bhodrolok. An honest man is safe here, outside his life is hell. The jail is much better for a poor man. Outside the jail, you can die on the pavement. No one will care. Here, if you say you won't eat, the guard will beat you up and force you. Might even shove a pipe up your nose. Three meals a day assured. Plus a roof, no rain, a blanket in winter. Try sleeping on a platform. No peace. The public will abuse you and kick you. The police will drive you away. Even falling ill here is better. They'll give you a pill. Outside? Nothing. So many dying right in front of hospitals. Without treatment. If someone beats you up here you can complain to jelaar shaheb or jomadar shaheb. The guilty are punished. No one listens to your complaint outside. Might is right. No one will show you any kindness or spare you. The weaker you are, the worse it is for you.'

The fine picture of the world outside jail that Imaan had woven in his head was shred to pieces. He concluded that the world on the other side of the tall walls was neither hospitable nor beautiful—not fit for human habitation. Apprehensively, he asked, 'Why does anyone live in such a dreadful place? Why don't they run away?'

When the man replied, despair was written all over his face, the way it is on the body of a prisoner on death row, whose final appeal for mercy has been rejected by the president. 'Where will they run away, bhai? The sea on one side, mountains on the other, deserts on a third, and the military on the fourth, who will kill first and talk later. Where is a man to go? How will he look for a better place?'

He wasn't a beggar by birth but because of circumstances. Classic beggars weep outside front doors, shouting, 'Maago, not eaten in two days, give me your stale rutis.' Those forced into this line by circumstances cannot do this. They wait at railway stations and bus-stands in search of passengers with kind faces, to whom they go up and say, 'I'm in trouble, lost my purse. Can't buy a ticket to get home. Can I please have ten rupees?' He's still begging, but from behind the fig-leaf of self-respect.

Just when Imaan's desire to enter the outside world was almost dead because of what the beggar had said, someone else spoke up. 'There's just one exit out of jail, but hundreds of entrances. Go find out what it's like out there. If you don't feel like staying, just use one of those doors to return. Free food, shelter and comfort again!'

'I don't know how to come back.'

'Nothing to know, no effort needed. Just get into a train. A week to ten days in jail if the checker catches you without a ticket. Get caught with your hand in someone else's pocket and you're assured of food for three months.'

This particular man came into jail at regular intervals, staying nine or ten days each time. Imaan had seen him at least half a dozen times. He had told Imaan that there were some twenty drinking dives in his neighbourhood, which were routinely raided every month. Before every raid, the excise department officials sent word to the owners, reminding them to have a scapegoat ready for arrest. The department had a monthly target of the number of people to be arrested and sent to court. These were the hazards that came with the job—the rules had to be followed. But the dive owners who paid them bribes also had to be protected. This man was a railway porter who sometimes served time in jail on behalf of one of the owners of drinking dives. He was paid for it; the dive owners had calculated it was cheaper to give him a wage for going to jail than to pay a fine.

And so, Imaan had decided he would at least pay one visit to the world outside, much as village people throng to the city to gape at the sights, while city people go to the seaside and the mountains. He wanted to verify all the stories he had heard. He had been waiting to turn sixteen-and-a-half, the age at which he was supposed to be released.

That day had passed a long time ago, but in the absence of anyone to plead his case, his file had remained at the bottom of the heap. Imaan was neither smart nor bold enough to go up to the jailer or the jail superintendent with a request to look into his case. All he could do was whine before the guards and jomadars, 'When will I be released?'

'As soon as it's time,' they would say, 'what's the hurry? You're getting three meals a day, no work, just wait. You'll find yourself free one of these days.'

A prisoner sentenced to death usually screams and shouts and flails his arms and legs when brought out of the condemned cell, before turning inert when he realises this is the end. So too did Imaan quieten down, knowing that release was distant, that protests would not help. Wake up, headcount, brush your teeth with ash, go to the toilet, collect breakfast, eat breakfast, have a bath, wander about, have lunch, headcount, nap, another headcount, dinner before darkness falls, return to the ward, final headcount of the day—he locked himself into the daily routine all over again. The days went by this way.

Then a journalist, arrested for some misdemeanour, came to jail. He learnt of the teenager named Imaan, forsaken by fate, who had been rotting in jail his entire life without having committed a crime. Securing bail after a week, he wrote a report sharply attacking the inhuman system of justice that had led to this. Published in the most circulated newspaper of the state, it evoked cries of condemnation from everyone, which even reached the ears of the sleeping administration, and forced the faded file from the bottom of the pile to rise to the top. It sailed swiftly from one desk to the next, and finally arrived, after collecting many signatures from various departments, at the jailer's desk. The magistrate had ordered Imaan Ali to be released with his honour intact as quickly as possible. The jailer had received the documents at about four in the afternoon, and signed them at once. Which was why the raaitar was now looking for Imaan to pass on the good news.

Imaan's friend Cartoon (who had been given that name by the deputy jailer)—skinny, with a mahogany complexion, two enormous protruding teeth, and three RPF cases against him—raced upstairs and dragged Imaan to his feet from his bed to tell him, 'Cock plugging your ear? Can't you hear them call you? *Khallas hukum* is here. Go see the raaitar quickly.'

'Are you sure it's me they are calling?' Imaan still couldn't quite believe it.

'Yes, you cocksucker,' Cartoon said with emphasis, 'it's definitely you.'

Following Cartoon's instructions, Imaan went up to the raaitar, who was so fed up by now, after having called out Imaan's name so many times, that he slapped him at once.

'Do you know how long I've been screaming your name, maadarchod?'

But not even the stinging slap that came with this scolding could make Imaan feel bad now, for the raaitar was saying, 'You'll be free tomorrow. You could have been free today if you'd turned up earlier.'

The siren had been rung for lockup, and everything was closed for the day. Cartoon had followed Imaan from the ward to the iron railing around the kestebil, but he hadn't been able to go farther because a guard was stationed on the spot. He was gazing at Imaan with tears in his eyes. They had become close friends, sharing their joys and sorrows, ups and downs, over the past two years. Now, with one of them leaving, their friendship would end. The news of Imaan's release was making Cartoon as sad now as it had made him happy earlier. 'Train friends part at the station, jail friends part at the gate.' An old prison saying. A friend who will throw his body between you and the guard's baton is someone you might never see again once you're free. Cartoon knew as much from his own experience, so why blame others? The last time he had got out of jail, he had never returned to visit his friends here despite promises. Today, he felt he should have.

But now he was both delighted and depressed to see Imaan returning towards him. 'What is it?' he asked, disappointment balled up in his throat. 'Why didn't they let you go? What did the raaitar say?'

'Tomorrow.' Imaan spat the word out like a glob of saliva. He was bubbling with confidence now.

'They're letting you go, right?'

'That's what he said.'

'Just one more night then. If they've said they'll release you, then they will.'

They entered the ward together. The headcount jomadar came a little later. The brass padlock was put on the gate once he left. Now the old inmates of the chhokra file gathered around Imaan. The good news had spread like wildfire: our Imaan is leaving tomorrow.

A young man named Komol occupied a corner of the northern end of the ward. A round face, curly hair, fair skin, loveable eyes. He had been here for eight months now, convicted for theft. He had stolen the cashbox from a grocery store where he worked and taken it home, where the police arrested him. Criminals who don't confess even after being beaten up by people or by the police don't hide the truth when in jail. Komol had said, 'I did steal it. But I was out of luck, and so I got caught. Four thousand, mairi. I'd have bought my dadababu a cycle if the police hadn't got me. We were supposed to have given it to him when he married my sister, but we couldn't. He beats up Didi because he didn't get the cycle. She'd have been saved if I could have got it for him.'

'He beats her up just for a cycle?'

'It's not just.' Komol seemed not angry but sympathetic to his brother-in-law. 'Dadababu has to travel seven or eight miles early in the morning to weigh fish in the wholesale market. There are no buses at that hour, and then he limps a little too, he can't walk all the way. So he'd said at the wedding, whether you can manage anything else or not, get me a cycle. We had said, we can't get you one before the wedding, but definitely within a month. If only I'd known that ...'

What he hadn't known was how difficult it would be to get hold of the money for a cycle. For someone who was barely able to make ends meet in his own family, the main objective of getting married was to get a Raleigh cycle, which he could ride to nearby villages and sell fish and then make enough money to maintain a wife. Naturally, he would lose his head if he didn't get his cycle as promised.

Now, rising from his corner, Komol went up to Imaan. After some hesitation, he asked, 'You don't have anyone of your own outside, do you? Where will you go, where will you live, what will you eat?'

'I know nothing about what's out there,' said Imaan. 'Let me get out first, I'll figure it out after that. One step at a time.'

'Pay a visit to Mohonpur if possible,' pleaded Komol. 'It's not a long walk, the house is quite close to the station. Will you go? It'll be of great help. My parents are wonderful people, they'll take care of you. Tell them to have me released. Any lawyer can get me bail. Tell them to get me bail, even if it means selling everything at home. Once I'm outside, I can buy it all again. It's been eight months—I can't stay here anymore.'

Komol was telling Imaan of his suffering—it was like complaining of a common cold to a cancer patient. But Imaan said nothing, he only listened in silence.

'Tell them, if necessary they can pawn the two kaathas of land in Chorki Malek's big yard to Gaya Das. I'll get it back when I get out. Tell them I'll die in jail if they don't have me released.'

'What does your father do?'

'Both my parents roll bidis. They get paid by the thousand.'

'How many brothers and sisters?'

'Two sisters, I'm in the middle.'

After a pause, he continued, 'I'd thought of finding a boy for my younger sister once Didi's problem was settled. But that ...' Komol trailed off into silence.

A little later, Imaan told him, 'I don't know what the future holds, but I'll try to go to your house.'

Cartoon was surprised by Komol's story, realising he had been deprived of justice and compassion.

When Cartoon was eleven or twelve, he used to live near the Kalighat temple. There were a dozen other boys like him there—orphans, runaways, persecuted by parents, dumped by relatives. They would cluster around the devotees like the older, crippled beggars, asking for money, but also making off with it sometimes, if they got the chance.

Once, the police from Kalighat police station took away five or six of them. They wanted their names and addresses before packing them off to jail. So a police officer seated behind a desk was asking for their fathers' names. In terms of caste and religion, some of them were Kaora Bagdis, some Muslims, some Namashudras. One of the boys said his name was Shadhon Chakraborty. Cartoon and his group didn't care about surnames. They all lived on the same pavement, their existence beset by the same problems.

But the officer was startled. 'You're a Braahmon!' Shadhon nodded in agreement. The officer leapt out of his chair, took a cane leaning against the wall and began to beat the other boys with it, roaring, 'You fucking thieves, you'll die on the same pavement you were born on. It wasn't enough to live like dogs, you had to drag a Braahmon boy into it, too, and turn him into a thief. He's going to hell because of you.'

The officer took the initiative to send Shadhon to a remedial home so that he could get an education and reintegrate into society. The others were despatched to Mallik Fatak Jail, where they would serve their sentences before returning to the pavement.

Cartoon felt that as the son of a Brahmin, Komol deserved the same consideration. A couple of slaps and he could have been set free instead of being sent to jail.

It was natural that Imaan wouldn't be sleeping tonight. When the night ended, the gong at the front gate was sounded five times as usual, followed the next moment by a grotesque shout. 'File! File!' Waking up with sleep-laden eyes, the prisoners squatted in pairs in long rows, exactly in the manner in which people squatted to shit in forests, without their buttocks touching the ground, their weight balanced on their feet. File-sitting, it was called.

A guard came a little later, unlocking the enormous padlock on the iron gate. The jomadar came in with his notebook and pen tucked beneath his arm to do the headcount and confirm that no one had escaped. The count tallied with yesterday's; no one had come in or left. The siren at the gate rang out after he gave the signal to the jail authorities. Yesterday had passed uneventfully, and an uncertain new day was about to begin.

The ward gates were opened wide a little later, with all the convicts being allowed to step outside. Imaan stepped out, too, like he did every day, followed by the usual routine of toilet, collecting ashes from the clay oven to brush his teeth, and then a breakfast of boiled chickpeas. After this came the resonant cry in the confined space: Imaan Aliiiiiii ...

His heart thumping loudly, a fearful Imaan Ali walked up to the kestebil. 'I'm Imaan Ali, saar.'

'Father's name?'

'Don't know. Mother's name Zahura Bibi.'

This raaitar's name was Poresh. Convicted of rape, he had been here two years. An educated young man, he had managed to lose his head and rape a woman. Of course, the full evidence would be available only once the trial began, since it would inevitably be insinuated that the young widow from the neighbourhood had actually seduced Poresh. For now, he was a prisoner under trial, working as a raaitar out of choice to pass the time.

Poresh walked Imaan to the jail office, to the desk of the bald deputy jailer, who was sitting there with Imaan and Zahura Bibi's faded, dust-covered file in front of him. The deputy jailer added some notes, and then took prints of all five of Imaan's fingers. Then, stamping a seal on his left wrist, he sent Imaan off to the guard on duty at the gate. 'Release this one first, special case, the newspapers have been writing about him.' And so, he was being let out before everyone else; the others who were due to be freed today would walk out half an hour later. As instructed, the guard on duty at the main gate unlocked a small gate at the side and shoved Imaan out. 'There! Pray to God you never have to come back here.'

The bright morning sunshine seemed to bathe Imaan in a glow as soon as he stepped into the free world outside the gate. A breeze sprung up to kiss his face. Imaan felt he had been reborn, and was taking his first step out of the safety of his mother's protection to enter a new land. This space was unfamiliar. All those creatures he could see in the distance—he had no idea whether they would help him to his feet if he slipped and fell, or whether they would knock him to the ground. All was unknown, everything a source of fear.

Another gate stood a few yards away from the main one, walking out of which would take Imaan beyond the jail limits, into the battlefield, where he would have to fight every minute just to survive, where no one yielded even an inch to anyone else, where every breath had to be nurtured with care.

Friends and relatives of those who were to be released a little later were gathered around the outer gate, anxiety written large on their faces. Each passing moment was like a century to them. Many of their hearts were quaking with fear; what if the last yard proved as long as a thousand miles? It had often happened that a prisoner had been given bail and all the conditions for release fulfilled, only for their relatives to see them being handcuffed at the gate by policemen from another jurisdiction and being taken away, rearrested, in legal terms.

There was no chance of something like this happening to Imaan. But there were no friends or family waiting for him outside the gate either. Not even the journalist who had played a crucial role in securing his release was there—he had seen the newsworthiness of Imaan's predicament, written about it, been paid for it, and moved on in search of other news reports that could bring him more money. He, too, had to deal with his children's school fees, his mother's rheumatism, his father's dental problems, new clothes for his family; where was the time to wait at the jail gate?

Had Imaan been a criminal instead of an innocent person, had he been serving a sentence all these years after being pronounced guilty, he would have left today with a good deal of money. Prisoners in jail are paid a small salary for the work they do, which, though paltry, adds up to a reasonable amount when it's time to leave, ten or twenty years later. But because he had not been convicted of any crime, all that Imaan had got was a stamp on his wrist. As long as it remained there, he would be allowed to ride on trams and buses without paying a fare.

Not that he hadn't got any money at all—he had twenty rupees, which Gobindo Das, the aged guard on duty at the gate, had given him from his own pocket. The man who had the contract for supplying vegetables to the jail gave the guard on gate duty twenty rupees every day—it had gone to Gobindo Das today. The primary condition for getting money was that the stale and damaged vegetables had to be ignored and not rejected when they were weighed at the gate. No one spotted them—not even the jailer or deputy jailer. And everyone received appropriate compensation for this. A hundred for the jailer, fifty for his deputy, twenty for the guard. But the jailer and deputy jailer were paid only once a month, while the guard was paid every day, since a different person was on duty each time.

Today Gobindo Das had pressed his twenty-rupee note into Imaan's hand, saying, 'Bad money for a good cause for once.'

The stamp on Imaan's wrist said Alipore Central Jail in English. It would take care of his transport for several days, while twenty rupees would last him, if he was thrifty, two days. Imaan had no idea that in just forty-eight hours, he would be facing doomsday, that he would be confronted with hunger and starvation.

Leaving the jail behind him, Imaan walked on. The compass would say he was going northwards. Leaving all his uncertainties behind, Imaan went in search of his true north.

2

The first two trains of the day cut through the darkness as they thundered towards the metropolis from south Bengal, the noise waking up the sleeping city. One of them was known as the 'fish train' and the other, the 'maid train'. The fish train was loaded with covered baskets filled with a variety of fish caught by villagers from streams and rivers, lakes and ponds, fisheries and the sea, meant to nurture the health and the palate of the residents of Calcutta. Rui, katla, bowaal, puti, tyangra, showl, ilish, koi, magur, telapia—a multitude of names. And the maid train was filled with young girls and married women from those same villages, on their way to the houses of the babus to mop the floors, do the dishes, wash the clothes, and perform a hundred other tasks.

The two trains stopped briefly at this station to belch out a number of people of different ages before proceeding as usual towards the heart of Calcutta. Some others had been waiting for these passengers: the rickshaw-drivers and porters, labourers and teashop owners, whose livelihood was linked to the movement of trains, and whose stomachs were filled only when the iron wheels rolled.

With the arrival of the trains, a busy day began, as always. And immediately afterwards, a voice as sharp as a train whistle became audible—‘*Ogo Giril-er baap*, where have you gone, why have you left this unfortunate woman alone in this cruel world?’

The sun hadn’t risen yet; the eastern sky had barely been tinged with red. The high-pitched wailing cut through the greyness, starting in no. 2 rail bosti, grazing the heads of the tiny shacks, and arrowing towards the station. No one else possessed this kind of a voice hereabouts. Everyone realised it was Aamodibala mourning her husband, who had just died. The same husband who had tormented her all their married life. And yet the irony of it was that she had to cry for him now at the top of her voice for fear of being shamed by everyone else if she did not.

Even a few days ago, before he had taken to his bed, the man would come home drunk every night and beat her up. After all these years of consuming alcohol, it was the alcohol that had consumed him. Back then, Aamodi had screamed at him a thousand times, ‘Die, die, you bastard, release me.’ Now that he was dead, she was feeling much lighter, much less burdened. And yet something was pricking at her heart, which was why Bhegai, Gogon and Bishnu, who were sleeping on platform no. 2, were jolted awake by her harsh wailing at dawn. Some of the hooch supplied by Charan that they had drunk with chicken drumsticks last night was still frothing in their bellies. It would continue to do what it was supposed to till it was expelled through the urinary tract. And so, the languorous haze still clung to their bodies. It would have been pleasant not to wake up so soon. However, they had no choice but to abandon their beauty sleep. This was no time for laziness, for an opportunity for making some cash was here, as the loud mourning signalled. And so they shook off their lethargy and got to their feet.

Everyone knew Jongol Poramanik was going to kick the bucket. He had ruined his liver himself with his constant drinking. Still, he had fought grimly with death for a full five and a half months even after the renowned doctor from KPC Hospital, who charged ten rupees per visit, had given up on him.

The first to abandon the comfortable bed on the platform was Gogon. He hustled the other two, 'Get up, quick. We need to go at once. The fucker's died finally, or that whore Aamodi wouldn't be squealing like a pig. Come on, don't waste time.' The reference to a squealing pig wasn't right, however, for the sound that the pigs made when slaughtered by the cleaners at KPC Hospital was far more grotesque. Unbearable. There was a tune, a rhythm, to Aamodi's wailing. Just like music, crying had its own melody and beat, tempo and metre. It wouldn't appeal to the heart unless these elements came together perfectly. Aamodi's dialogue delivery was quite appropriate in this regard.

It was the rule to lament a near-one's death. Otherwise, the soul could not rest in peace. Moreover, people said vicious things. '*Ki niddoy maagi re mairi!* The bitch is so heartless she didn't shed a single tear when her man died.' And so, Aamodi had flung herself to the floor, flailing her limbs as she wept helplessly, faithfully copying all the heartbreaking scenes she had seen in movies.

Jongol Poramanik was not the kind of person Aamodi should have been shedding tears for. It wasn't just the fact that he used to beat her up on any pretext. After all, there was no house in the slum where a man didn't beat his wife. The only exceptions were those men whose wives beat them. So Aamodi had accepted this. But what she couldn't put up with was his womanising. There was no counting the number of times during their seven or eight years of married life that he had brought a woman into their shanty and taken her to bed with Aamodi watching. He would fetch someone from the station and throw his wife out. 'Go sleep somewhere else, come back in the morning.' That was when she had cursed him repeatedly. 'Die, you bastard, die. I'm pledging a rupee and a quarter for Ma Shetala if only you die of cholera.'

On some nights, when he had passed out from drunkenness, Aamodi had even considered dragging him to the railway lines and dumping him there. No one would suspect anything, so many people were killed this way. An hour of weeping in the morning, and she'd be relieved of all the trouble.

Eventually, she hadn't had to do it herself; God had listened to her prayers and taken on the responsibility. Aamodi was free now, except that she'd have to maintain social mores by crying and fainting once or twice, or else people would say terrible things.

Aamodi had known that the day for tears wasn't too far away. Once the doctor had said there was nothing more to be done, she had begun to picture the whole thing in her head. The crying scene that had caught her fancy was from the play *Behula's Journey*, where Behula wept buckets with her arms around Lakhinder after his death. But on thinking it over, she had decided that although the tune and dialogue were appealing and it worked on the stage, it would not fit in here. So she had been watching out for which of her neighbours could cry well enough to keep everyone engaged, paying careful attention when Ponchu khuro or Gopen or Hashi mashi from the rail bosti had died. It was paying off today. Anyone who heard her wails, accompanied by carefully curated excerpts from three different dialogues expressing grief, embellished by lines of her own, had to admit this was what mourning should be like. It was worth dying twice over if it could provoke such lamentation.

And so, Aamodi emitted another shriek, '*Ogo paanonath, o my dalling*, if this was what you had in mind, why didn't you kill me first! Your absence has left me with a dead soul in a living body!'

Her neighbour Shudashi had captivated onlookers with the same words and cadences when she had become Ponchu Nayek's freshly minted widow. Many still remembered her spectacular mourning.

Aamodi's renewed crying left Gogon, Bhegai and Bishnu in no doubt that it was time to step up to the task. The noble responsibility of fulfilling their duty, for which they had been born, for which they lived, had sent its summons. Even from this distance they could hear the stricken voice, 'There's no one I can call my own on a day like this. Who will I turn to for help? Who will rescue me?'

The plastic sheet on which these three men had been sleeping had, till yesterday, been the property of a rickshaw-driver, who would put it up in front of the passenger seat to shield his passengers from the rain. But he was no longer its owner. Folding it and stashing it away in a secret corner of the platform, Bhegai smiled, saying to himself: 'This'll come in useful again tonight unless someone steals from the thief.' Turning to his companions, he said, 'Are you going right now? I need a shit. Go on ahead, or wait if you can. I'll take a dump quickly and come back.'

Gogon, who had woken up before the rest and then shaken them awake, sounded irritated. 'Can't you hold it in? Let's finish our work. Then you can shit your heart out.'

Lighting a bidi, Bhegai took a long drag and emitted a mouthful of smoke. 'There's no telling how long it'll take. Might get stuck, it'll take hours then. How can I hold it in so long? Give me a minute, I'll just go behind the cabin, and be back in no time.'

Gogon grimaced. 'Behind the cabin! Your shit will freeze if Pellad babu is there. He'll pour dirty water on your head if he sees you.'

There was a dense growth of morning glory creepers behind the signalling cabin, which was where ordinary people urinated and defecated. Next to it was a pond, its smelly water a putrid blue in colour. Shit in the bushes and wash up in the pond—that had been the long-standing practice here. But the cabin officer had been creating problems of late. There was a southerly breeze these days, bringing with it the stench of human excretion, making it difficult to remain inside the cabin. Prahlad babu had warned everyone a few days ago not to do 'those things' anymore over there, but with no one paying any attention, he had turned aggressive. The moment he saw anyone squatting to defecate, he poured a bucket of water on them from the first floor.

Even though this was how people used the morning glory bushes in the daytime, this changed in the evening. No one was desperate to go in there anymore after dark, for fear of their lives, since there was a good chance of being bitten by snakes or scorpions. They did their job directly on the wooden sleepers of the railway tracks. Of course, there was the occasional passer-by, but those who walked and those who squatted maintained the norms of peaceful cohabitation.

When the night grew deeper, the area was taken over by the low-priced sex workers at the station. Their customers were even more withered than they were. There were easy options for entertainment-seekers among the poor to rent cheap rooms by the hour at Diamond Harbour or Ghutiari Sharif. But these customers were so impoverished that even if they could somehow manage to meet the price charged by a sex worker, they could not afford to rent a room. So they were forced to risk their lives and make use of the bushes. But even if they didn't fear snakes and scorpions, it was impossible to tell in the dark where people had chosen to defecate earlier in the day. Kobita had once found her entire back smeared with worm-infested faeces. These days Shondhya, Shobita, Kobita, Maloti and the rest of them carried a plastic sheet to lie on, which they washed in the pond after every use.

Right now, though, Bishnu hustled Bhegai, 'Stop talking and do your stuff quickly. There'll be a screw-up if Shiben and Netai from no. 1 get there before us. We'll get fuck all.'

'Is that so easy?' About to leave, Bhegai stopped and turned back. 'Do we ever go to no. 1? You think we'll leave them alone if they create trouble in our area? We'll beat them up. I don't care what happens after that. Stick to your own area, don't get into someone else's.' Bhegai tarried no longer; things were getting dire.

Bishnu sauntered up to the tea-stall on the platform. Kali Boshak, the owner, who knew them well, looked at him suspiciously, his eyes radiating revulsion. 'What do you want?'

'Two teas and a bundle of Lal Shuto bidi,' said Bishnu.

'Get a matchbox too,' Gogon told him.

'No credit first thing in the morning, I'm letting you know right now,' said Kali Boshak sternly.

Summoning up a pinched expression of victimhood, Bishnu said, 'Who's asking for credit? Did I mention credit?'

'Just letting you know in advance,' said Kali Boshak as impatiently as earlier. 'What if you drink your tea and then say you have no cash? I can't squeeze it back out of you, can I?'

Standing up in support of his beleaguered friend, Gogon said, 'Why'd we ask for tea if we couldn't pay?'

'As if you haven't earlier,' hissed Kali Boshak. 'Don't you talk, Gogon. Remember how you ran away after drinking your tea and eating a bun? I had to chase you.'

'When?'

'Try to remember. You shouldn't have a problem recollecting.'

Gogon remembered. He was famished that day but had no money, and no one was going to give him food on credit either, since he already owed everyone a good deal of money. Gogon was terrified, for he knew that his hunger would mount as the day went by, and his body would turn limp like a dead fish by the late afternoon. He wouldn't have enough strength to even stand on his feet, and would have to lie down in a corner of the platform by the time night fell. His vision would blur, his limbs would start trembling, his head would start spinning, a storm would rage in his chest, and then his eyes would slowly close, sending him into eternal sleep. So Gogon had decided to take a chance just so he could survive.

Embarrassed by the recollection, he smiled ruefully. 'I'm not the same Gogon anymore,' he said. 'I had no work or money then, but I have a business now. One round with a sack and I can make enough money to maintain a bitch and screw a whore on the side.'

These were the precise words with which Kawar had initiated him into this business. 'Stop fucking around, pick up a sack. One round will get you enough for a wife and a whore.' Many people had often said that Calcutta's streets were lined with money, but no one had ever gone into it deeply enough. Gogon had the answer now. Torn rubber slippers, ordinary plastic bags, discarded water bottles—everything that people threw away as rubbish was in fact valuable. They could not only pay for his meals, but also for his liquor.

Kali Boshak filled two cups of tea from the kettle without wasting more words. Holding out a bundle of bidis, he said, 'Fifteen bucks! Out with it!'

'Are you at least going to let me have my tea or not?' said a peeved Gogon.

Kali Boshak didn't respond but kept a strict eye on them.

Finishing his tea, Bishnu fished out two ten-rupee coins from the folds of his lungi and handed them over, saying in the same tone, 'Five bucks back!'

Kali Boshak slammed a five-rupee coin down on a high shelf. Bishnu was tucking it back into his lungi when Bhegai returned with an abashed smile. 'My goddamn belly was troubling me, but it's better now.' This was followed by a resentful 'What's this—you had your tea without me? Hard-hearted bastards. Come on, get me a cup.'

Bishnu looked at him angrily. 'Are you going to sponge off me all your life? I'm bankrupt, thanks to you. The booze last night, the snacks—you didn't pay for any of it. And now the tea, too. What's going to happen the rest of the day?'

A deflated Bhegai said, 'Don't talk of sponging—it's painful. I ask you because you're a friend with an income, you can afford to spend a little on us. If you don't want to, just say so. But if you talk to me like that, I'm never asking you again. Fuck this liquor—in through the mouth, piss twice, and it's all gone.'

'Enough of the drama,' Bishnu scolded Bhegai. 'Finish your tea quickly. Let's go find out what we can do with Jongol Poramanik's case.'

Aamodi had finally stopped crying and was lying in a dead faint, as the rules demanded. It was necessary to get some rest so that she could resume with renewed vigour after a while. Following the same rules, a neighbour whose husband had also died was sprinkling water on her face, saying, 'He had to go, he's gone, but you're here. Don't cry anymore, be strong. You have a child. You have to hold back your grief for his sake.' She was repeating verbatim what she had been told. This was how the wheel went round, for better or for worse.

Bishnu, Bhegai and Gogon started walking along the railway tracks towards no. 2 rail bosti, which was not far from the station. It began at the signal post on the tracks that streaked from west to east like an arrow. To the north of the tracks, after a small clearing which turned into a temporary market every evening, stood the shanties of no. 1 bosti; the number having been acquired by virtue of being the first settlement here. But no. 2 bosti had a far higher population.

Since it was morning, the residents of the numerous huts to the right of the railway lines, just after the end of platform no. 1, had quite justifiably claimed their rights to squatting in the clearing across the tracks to move their bowels. Behind them was a large moss-covered pond, and, beyond it, the road, lined with small shops.

Those defecating here pretended that anyone walking along the railway lines was blind. Not that they were wrong, for no one could indeed see them, as no one so much as cast a glance their way, or, even if they did, looked away at once. No one wants to see rows of bare buttocks when starting their day.

Bhegai remembered coming here one morning as a young boy, along with several other imps just like him, to chuck stones and jeer at those shitting here. Incensed, Palan-er baap had shot to his feet, lifting his lungi and shouting, 'Come on, you sons of bitches, throw your stones right here!'

Right now, a stream of train passengers were walking along the tracks towards the road on the right that would take them to the Bagha Jatin crossroad. All of them were daily labourers and porters, also known by another identity—chhotolok, the lowborn.

Perhaps it was because they were the lowborn that they had taken this route, for the bhodrolok, the highborn genteel classes, did not often walk this way, and certainly not at this dangerous hour. The sharp acidic tang of turds and piss was snapping at everyone's nostrils, forcing them to cover their mouths and noses and hurry along as quickly as possible.

There was another route from the station to the Bagha Jatin crossroad, via the bus-stop, which meant a walk of at least three miles, twice as long as this short-cut. Labourers and porters would, in any case, be putting in physical work all day long; they didn't want to expend their energy unnecessarily first thing in the morning.

Gogon, Bhegai and Bishnu were also walking along the railway tracks, their eyes narrowed like that of predators. Once the platform ended, the right-hand side of the railway lines was an endless sea of tiny shanties built with rotting leaves, scraps of wood and gunny sheets, erected on stilts, and stuck to one another in a way that left no scope for privacy. The inhabitants of one hut could feel the neighbouring one shaking in the middle of the night and know what was going on.

The residents of the rail bosti could not go to sleep till the last train in both directions, up and down, had gone by. Even if they did fall asleep, the last train woke them up as it passed, shaking the ground and whistling grotesquely.

There was a story about a village where every family had nine or ten children, while the other villages around it had the usual one or two. Investigations revealed that a railway line went past the village, along which a train passed at top speed at two in the morning. Woken up abruptly, couples would have sex in a bid to tire themselves out so that they could go back to sleep.

In the rail bosti, the shaking of one shanty stirred the hearts and bodies living in the neighbouring shanties, whose shaking then aroused those who lived on the other side.

On the northern side of the railway lines, a mossy lake ran for about a quarter of a mile from the end of platform no. 2—it had probably been created when the soil was dug out to raise the base for the rail tracks. Beyond it lay a patch of land on which nine or ten shacks had been put up. Scattered around the edge of the lake, and reached by walking down the slope from the railway line, they represented the beginning of the settlement known as no. 2 rail bosti, which had been turned upside down this morning by grief.

All the residents here were among the poorest of the poor, working-class people from the lowest strata. Among the men, some pedalled rickshaws, some pulled hand-drawn carts to transport goods, some were porters, and some worked as daily labourers. All the women worked as maids in the houses of the affluent. Neither birth nor death was an occasion for great celebration or mourning, for life itself was like the camel's hump, or the shell on the snail's back, an immovable burden that had to be carried, and which offered nothing but pain. The only desire of their lives was to lighten this load in any manner possible. They had no time to pay attention to anything else in the world.

Aamodi had finally decided to regain consciousness. How long can you go on having water splashed on your face? The person splashing water knew it had to start gently and then gather pace. The water had to be hurled from one's cupped palm towards the eyes of the target from a distance of two or three feet, four or five times in succession. Only then would it work.

'What's the use of crying,' everyone consoled Aamodi as they tried to edge out and go to work. 'You'll only end up falling sick yourself, but the one who's gone won't come back.' No one was particularly concerned about Jongol Poramanik; a dead man needed no attention. All that remained to think about was his cremation, which someone or the other would cheerfully volunteer to take care of. The dead were more valuable than the living in this slum.

Moharaj lived with his wife Ranibala and two children in a hut on the edge of the railway line, at the head of the path that led to Jongol Poramanik's shanty. The children were entirely Ranibala's doing—Moharaj could claim no credit here. She had carried them in her womb, given birth to them, and fed them. Both the boys were still young, but very naughty, always up to mischief. And yet if Moharaj were to assert a misplaced right over Ram and Baloram as their father and slap them around a little, Ranibala pounced on him like a tigress—'I'm warning you, don't you touch my kids. You're just a turd whom I allow in the veranda. Even if their real father, who used his thing, tries to beat them, I'll break his arm. I carried them for nine months, I feed them every day—if anyone has to beat them, it'll be me. How dare you even try? Do you pay for their food and clothing?'

It was true that unlike others who had lured women into their homes with promises of fine clothes and money, Moharaj had actually married Ranibala before having his way with her. Winning her heart with his words, buying her bangles and ribbons, a twenty-eight-year-old Moharaj had persuaded a sixteen-year-old Ranibala to run away with him, after which he had married her here on the railway tracks with sidoor and white bangles. His voice thick with emotion, he had said, 'I swear by the gods you are my wife from today. The past is past; I shall never look at anyone else, never mention anyone else. You are my wife now. For better or for worse, our lives will be one.'

Those were heady days of happiness. Ranibala used to work as a cook at a boarding house in South Park. Being pretty, she had had no problems getting the job. Even the shortcomings in her cooking were compensated for by the way she looked.

The boarders had come to the city from places so far away that hardly ever did any of them return home for the holidays. Some of them tried to go for the bird in the hand instead of the two in the bush by groping her and then adding a tip of a rupee or more. But the one who gave her the most money was Shaadhin Shorongi, a clerk at Adorsho Balika Bidyalay.

Before he paid, though, the fifty-five-year-old Shaadhin babu would run his hands over her body and face for quite some time, faint beads of perspiration appearing on his forehead. 'I have a daughter just like you, ma. Identical. The same nose ... see, this spot on your back ... give me your hand, yes ... the fingers are the same too.' As he spoke, he would touch Ranibala all over. 'That's why I look at you so often and kiss you like this. I'm a father after all, my heart aches for her. You mustn't mind—think of me as your own father.'

Moharaj used to work at One-Armed Paanu's scrapyard next to the railway siding. This was where everything discarded by people for being unusable was traded. All the iron scrap and bottles and old newspapers that ragpickers collected through the day were sold here. It was Moharaj's responsibility to check and measure and weigh everything that was bought.

There were two sides to the enterprise, one of which ran in full view of everyone and the other, away from prying eyes. The first operated by daylight and the second, in the dead of night. Under cover of night, a figure that had all but melted into the darkness would knock softly on the door, and Moharaj would open it as silently as a cat. That was when the clandestine material was delivered, ranging from motor parts and manhole covers to bearings from freight trains and copper wire. Paanu could even accommodate an entire truck or two if it was dismantled.

Several quintals of copper wire, stolen from a high-tension pole somewhere between two stations, had come in one drizzly night. The bark from banana trees had been laid out cleverly across the wires to stop the passage of electricity through them, after which they had been severed with the help of a wire-cutting instrument.

With the last train gone, there was no way to tell whether the overhead wires were live or not. Since the railway police on duty were doing everything but guard railway property, the thieves used their wire-cutter fearlessly to cut the wires into small lengths, stuffed them into gunny bags, and hid them in the bushes or inside a moss-covered pond. After the police had stopped searching and the commotion had died down, the wires were transported under cover of night to Paanu's junkyard.

Paanu, in fact, used to be an active member of just such a gang, its 'head mistri', as the chief workman was referred to. Once, when he was extracting the bearings from a freight car, the jack slipped and the carriage fell on his arm. He was not the only one to have lost an arm this way. It was a simple but risky operation—clamping the jack on the railway line to lift the carriage a few inches and extract the bearing with two fingers. There was no escape if the jack were to slip at that moment. It was only the two affected fingers that needed to be removed, but the doctor at the hospital inevitably amputated the arm from the elbow or wrist downwards.

After losing his arm and spending several months in jail, Paanu had no choice but to give up on this profession. Formerly known only as Paanu, he now became known in the neighbourhood as 'One-Armed Paanu'. It was after this that he had set up this business, turning from a sheyana into a khaau, from a master thief into a dealer.

Having worked in this line before, he was acquainted with all the sheyanas. Moreover, he had done time in their lair, where he had come to know those of them he hadn't met before. So his enterprise flourished. Like in every other business, Paanu's capital, too, was his honesty. Everyone trusted him enough to leave their stolen goods with him, which he then sold to suitable buyers and gave the thieves a fair price. He never cheated them. A portion of the takings had to be offered at the local police station too.

'So you've done some business,' the officer said, smiling.

'All with your blessings,' Paanu said deferentially.

'With whom?'

'Enjoy your mango, saar, don't ask where the tree is.'

'We'll find out anyway.'

'That's all right, but it would be wrong of me to disclose it.'

Paanu was on close terms with the police, but, as the saying goes, a policeman can never be family; he's perfectly capable of biting the hand that feeds him. And so, the very next morning, after Paanu had received the copper wire, a jeep filled with policemen drove up to his scrapyard. Given the location of the crime, the police knew exactly where the stolen goods would be found eventually. With their informers spread everywhere, they also knew who the thieves were. It was difficult to identify these sources. For all Paanu knew, it could be the driver of the rickshaw-trailer on which the wires had arrived.

Awbodh Shamonto, the paan-chewing second-in-command of the police station, was in the jeep. He was quite fond of Paanu, and was mortified to have to arrest him. Sadly, he said, 'I have no choice, you have no idea how much pressure there is on us. I won't keep my job without a few arrests. The order, in fact, was to stage an encounter. The DM is a very strict man who has said, catch them and shoot them; there is no other way to terrorise criminals. Let's see ... maybe one or two around the middle of the month.

But not you—you don't have to worry. Just arrange for some money, and I'll make sure the charges are light—you'll be released in a couple of years. But it's stolen property, I can't do less than that, I won't fool you. You've looked after me, I'll help you as much as I can.'

Moharaj went to jail, too, on the same charges. Shamonto babu had kept his word, and neither Moharaj nor Paanu had had to serve more than two years. Paanu was a good boss; he had not stinted on paying for Moharaj too. But the sentence came four years later, and they had had to spend that period in jail, too, as under-trial prisoners. When he came out after six years, Moharaj discovered that Ranibala had given birth to twins. And his shanty with walls of thatched bamboo had been replaced by a permanent structure with three-inch bricks. There wasn't even a stool to sit on earlier, and now there was a proper cot, on which the father of the children, Shaadhin Shorongi, was ensconced, sipping ginger tea.

Seeing Moharaj return, Shorongi said, 'I've done my duty. She's so young, where would she go, how would she survive. I've protected her to the best of my abilities. I'm getting on in years. I cannot support two households anymore. I'm glad you're back. It's your household, you can take charge now. You have my blessings.'

Ranibala was no longer the naive, helpless girl who had followed Moharaj from the Gobindopur rail colony—time had matured her. Even though Shaadhin Shorongi wanted to be free of his responsibilities, Ranibala was unwilling to release him. Let him remain. Moharaj wouldn't be able to pull off what she wanted. She needed Shaadhin babu to buy her a couple of kaathas of land near Piali. But wiser heads in the slum explained to her that you could call an ass your father if you were in trouble, but it wasn't right to call your father an ass. After all, Moharaj is your bhaatar, you're married to him, they told her. It was a relationship over seven lifetimes; it wasn't like a straw in the wind. Shaadhin would remain in Kolkata only as long as he had his clerk's job. As soon as he retired, he would run back to his hometown. Who was going to track him down in Medinipur after that? Don't drive Moharaj away because of him, they advised her. Let your babu stay here, but don't make Moharaj leave.

Despite the harmful proliferation of atheists, religiosity and morals had not yet been obliterated; right and wrong, piety and sin were seen deeply entrenched in the human mind. Ranibala believed in Hindu customs. She believed that her husband was her lord and master. The wife had to return to her husband to broadcast her chastity.

However, Ranibala was now faced with not one crisis but two. Her own problem was that she couldn't possibly have both men in her life. And second, allowing two men in the same house could lead to murder.

So Ranibala was forced to bid Shaadhin Shorongi a tearful goodbye. Escorting him to the station, she said, 'Don't forget us. Send money every month, I'll need it to bring the boys up. I'll come to your school if you don't send the money, don't forget that ...'

Shaadhin Shorongi had no difficulty identifying the threat. Recoiling, he said, 'Of course, I won't forget. I'll bring it myself at the beginning of every month and spend a little time with you. I can do that, can't I? I'd like to see the children too.'

'Have I ever said you mustn't?' Ranibala reassured him. 'The house is yours—come anytime you want to. I'll cook whatever you bring, I'll make whatever your heart desires. Such a long relationship can't just be ended abruptly.'

Moharaj was now attentively fulfilling his responsibility as a householder while running a business enterprise selling ganja. He had made convenient arrangements at home for smoking, keeping all his equipment in a wooden crate—the bong, hemp, a knife to slice the ganja, a piece of wood as a cutting tray.

A peculiar, stinging smell always swirled around the house, which also acted as an advertisement. Even a stranger who liked his weed could make out there was a dive here.

Moharaj had had to spend the night in the police lock-up after being arrested, and was taken to court only the next afternoon. After which, following conventions, the police asked that he be remanded for five days for interrogation. This was necessary, for there was the risk of being reprimanded by the court afterwards—why wasn't the accused questioned; he might have revealed the names of other criminals. That night, a loud commotion had woken Moharaj up at around 2:00 a.m. He could tell that someone was being beaten up mercilessly on the floor of the office outside, and the person was shrieking loudly.

One-Armed Paanu was sleeping next to Moharaj on a dusty blanket rolled out on an even dustier floor. 'They're beating someone up,' Moharaj had told him fearfully. Turning over on his side, Paanu had said, without missing a beat, 'Let them, what's your problem. Go back to sleep.'

Like a philosopher, he had added the hallowed saying, 'Eat fire, shit coal. That's how the world goes round.'

Still, Moharaj had tried to wake him up. It was his first time in a lock-up; he was terrified. 'Why are they beating him up like that?'

'Must have done something to deserve it,' Paanu had answered, without a change in tone.

'Who is it?'

'How should I know, I'm exactly where you are. What does it matter to us?'

'What if they beat us up too?' Moharaj had asked in panic.

'They won't,' Paanu had answered confidently, 'why should they? We've done as they had asked us to. We've paid every last paisa they demanded. They might have beaten us up if we'd been disobedient, but we haven't.' Illiterate, and therefore unaware that he was citing Isaac Newton, Paanu continued, 'The one who's doing the beating also suffers like the one being beaten up. I've seen Constable Modon pleading with the officer: "I've beaten up four of them, saar. It's someone else's turn now, my arms are aching." It's not very relaxing to beat people up.'

Moharaj hadn't been convinced. His heart was quaking, his body was covered with sweat. Rising to his feet, he went up to the locked door, and looked down the dark corridor leading away from the cell. The office was farther ahead, on the left. That was where the officers had their desks. Moharaj tried to gauge what was going on in there. The victim was shouting, 'I won't do it again, babu. Forgive me this time, I'll never do it again.' The stick continued to be smashed on his back, accompanied by angry growls. 'Why won't you do it again? Do it. Who's stopped you? But make sure we get our due. It's been six months—even patience has its limits.'

After this had gone on a long time, Moharaj realised that the man being beaten up ran a ganja dive. He used to work at a factory earlier, one of the thousands of factories that had closed down under the administration of the labourer- and peasant-friendly government, making two-hundred thousand workers jobless. The man had had no choice but to become a ganja dealer just to keep his family fed and clothed.

Selling ganja was not wrong, though, but not giving the police their cut from the monthly earnings was. This was the crime the man had committed over the past six or seven months. He had been evading the police, and hence this beating.

Moharaj wasn't going to be like him. After his release from jail, he went to meet the officer-in-charge at the local police station with the intention of starting a ganja dive of his own. 'I'm very poor, babu. I had to do time in jail because I worked for Paanu. But I'm innocent. I'm not going down that road again, for who knows what all might happen. Your kindness knows no bounds. Allow me to start a ganja thek in no. 2 rail bosti. If I can make money, some of it will go to you.'

With a beatific smile, the benevolent officer had said, 'Go into business honestly and fearlessly. Give me three hundred a month, make sure it gets to me by the 10th. That's the last date. You can use my name; no one will trouble you. God above and me below, we're there with you.'

Moharaj had been running his business with a shining reputation since then. Shaadhin babu had contributed the capital, along with, of course, the two-roomed house with three-inch bricks. No one else in the bosti had a house of bricks. Blood was thicker than water, after all. Whenever Shaadhin Shorongi missed Ram and Baloram, he came over for a visit. It wasn't possible to come during the day, for he had work then. So he came in the evening, staying the night and leaving early in the morning. Back when Moharaj had been in jail, Shaadhin babu used to visit during holidays, only to discover that the neighbours had their minds in the gutter—they peeped in through the bamboo walls and giggled all the time. Ranibala had admonished Shaadhin babu, 'I feel ashamed, don't you? What sort of a man are you? You work in a school, so many people know who you are—how can you stand their laughing at you?'

This was why Shaadhin babu had put up the brick walls and the tin roof. He could come and go whenever he pleased now, at any time of the day. The Peeping Toms were thwarted. A veranda ran in front of the two rooms, at the northern end of which Ranibala did the cooking, while Moharaj ran his business at the southern end. The house faced the railway line.

Shaadhin babu had an infirmity, the kind any elderly man could have. So he had to take a pill whenever he came here. The problem wasn't embarrassing, but buying the pill was. What would people think if they saw the revered head clerk of Adorsho Balika Bidyalay buying this particular medicine? His name would be ground into the dirt. So he'd send Moharaj to get it. 'Ask for three-nought-three capsules.

Will you remember the name or should I write it down for you? Ask for hundred mg.'

Shaadhin babu would take the medicine with warm milk in the afternoon or at night. He grew frisky soon afterwards. A little later, he would summon Ranibala. 'There's something I have to tell you.' One of the two rooms was earmarked for him. He would stay in it when he came; it remained locked the rest of the time. Ranibala kept the key, Shaadhin babu never took it. She'd go in there to find out what he had to tell her ...

Moharaj was sitting outside the locked door of that room now, smoking a bidi. Aamodi's shrieks had woken him up. Not just him but the entire slum. Still, he hadn't gone up to her door. Considering the reckless way she was crying, her clothes had to be in disarray. It was always thrilling to see a tempting female body, but now was not the time. So Moharaj decided that smoking was the wiser option.

Throwing away his bidi after a final drag, he glanced at the railway lines, where three figures were visible. 'Vultures flock around dead cows, and these shoytans turn up whenever a man dies,' Moharaj muttered angrily under his breath. 'The fucking bastards have arrived to devour Jongol Poramanik ...'

Now he felt it necessary to stand by the helpless and distressed Aamodi, so that no one could cheat the newly widowed young woman. Those swine were sure to give her a bad deal in her hour of grief. She couldn't possibly think for herself right now. Astuteness at this time was out of the question; she would say yes when she meant no, and forfeit what was hers by rights.

So Moharaj followed the three shadows to Aamodi's front door.

Exhausted from all her crying, she had no more tears to shed. All she could do was whimper melodramatically, 'How will I live now, how will my days and nights pass in your absence? Not a single person is left on this land to wipe my tears or to bring me home when I'm lost ...' Without missing a beat, she added, 'Giril, your uncles are here. They've travelled a long way, get them a mat to sit on.'

The three musketeers were pleased to see that mourning had not made Aamodi forget her manners. One of them piped up, 'No need for a mat or anything. We'll stand, we're fine standing. Cry as long as you want, let it all out. We'll talk business afterwards.'

'Any relatives nearby?' Moharaj asked Aamodi. 'Any way to let them know? Any chance they might turn up?'

'No relatives,' crooned Aamodi. 'All of them live on the other side of the Matla ...'

'Didn't some of them live in the Gopalpur bosti?'

'Used to, not anymore. All gone home. Sonnabitches in the mincipality evicted them.'

'I heard they were all shifted to Lobondanga or some place.'

'Not all. Only those who had voter cards and ration cards. My father and brother used to rent a shack. They had no papers. So they went back home—what else was there to do. My brother drives a rickshaw-trailer in Gosaba.'

'Who's going to go all the way to inform them? And even if they're told, how will they travel so far quickly? The earliest they can make it here is tomorrow. The corpse will rot. A rotting corpse brings bad luck,' said Moharaj.

Someone, or some people, had many years ago dumped Jongol hereabouts from a train one morning. His father or maybe his mother was the ringleader of a child-trafficking gang; no one knew for sure, though. Like they did from other villages, these gangs sometimes picked up children from the station here and supplied them to the Arab countries for camel races. Who knew, perhaps Jongol had been picked up for this very purpose from some distant village. Maybe the police had shown up, or something had gone wrong with their delivery, but they had abandoned him at the station. The station was generous, it gave shelter to many orphaned, helpless children. It gave birth to many too. And so, it had drawn Jongol into its arms, and the child had grown up amidst the crowd of the unwanted and the redundant. Starting out with begging, he had gone on to washing glasses at a drinking dive and then graduated to driving a rickshaw. He had sprouted like a weed and died as one. Few knew he had been alive all this time; fewer still had anything to gain or lose from his death. Birth and death were insignificant events in this railway slum.

Aamodi was moaning, 'All of you who live here are family, you tell me what I should do. No need to inform anyone else. No one checked on him when he was alive. Who needs them now that he's dead?'

The three musketeers realised that a conversation was looking feasible. Aamodi might be grief-stricken, but she hadn't lost her mind. She could hear, she could understand everything clearly. She was capable of taking decisions too.

After a pause Gogon said, speaking slowly, 'See, forget the fancy talk, let me get to the point. You know why we're here. We're the ones who take away the body no matter who dies. We get the last rites done. So are you willing to hand over Jongol-da's body to us? If you are, you have no further responsibilities—we'll take care of things. Flowers, incense, bier for the final journey—everything.'

Moharaj interrupted before Aamodi could reply, 'Obviously, the body has to go to someone for the last rites. Can't keep the corpse at home. Whether it's you or Nitai and Bhoben, it's all the same. But first, there's a matter that needs settling.' Moharaj looked around at the crowd that had gathered. 'What do all of you think?'

Bishnu was enraged at Moharaj's seizing the initiative. 'Who's going to do the talking,' he asked acidly, 'you?'

Moharaj was taken aback by this sudden attack. 'Why should it be me? The owner of the body will talk to you.'

'Then what are you butting in for? Shut up.'

'What kind of talk is this, Bishnu? All of us live here, together in happiness and in sorrow. Remember the floods? Aamodi had waist-high water in her shanty; didn't I let them stay in my house for three days? Ask her whether I charged for it.'

'Robbe Bagdi would have charged by the hour,' someone said in support of Moharaj.

Gogon said, 'Why bring Robbe into this? Renting his place out by the hour is his business. Ask him and he says his niece and her husband are visiting, or some village connection's son and daughter-in-law. All of them turn up at night and leave in the morning. We know what's going on, just that we don't say anything, and why should we? When no one else speaks up, why should we ask for trouble? Let them do whatever they want, none of my business.'

The sun was climbing, and with it, the heat. Those who wouldn't get a meal if they didn't work every day were disappointed by Jongol Poramanik's timing. You never knew, what if Aamodi insisted she wanted to cremate her husband herself? They wouldn't be able to refuse if she asked them for help, and that would be the end of their wages for the day. And of food too.

But now they were relieved that Gogon, Bishnu and Bhegai had appeared and seemed to be having a cordial exchange with Aamodi. These three would take care of the body, no one else would have to pitch in and lose a day's work. And so, the neighbours stepped up fearlessly to offer their condolences.

'He was a good man. Never thought he'd die this way, our Jongol, I'm so sad.' Passing on their brief consolations in the quickest possible time and at no cost, they left one by one to service their bellies. Some even took the opportunity to feel up Aamodi under the pretext of comforting her. 'Don't cry, Aamodi. Jongol may have gone, but I'm here. Just let me know if you need anything.'

Shibpodo worked at Komol Shamonto's potato godown. He had got married, but his wife had run away, leaving a child behind. He knew the agony of being alone, the sharpest bit being her absence in bed at night, when he simply couldn't sleep. Now it was Aamodi's turn to experience the same pain. Her heart would also twist in the dead of night. Shibpodo began to think ahead furiously—couldn't two lonely hearts come together now?

He decided not to go to work today, never mind the loss of a day's wages. He would stick by Aamodi. He would take the test of friendship in this troubled time for her and pass it with flying colours.

So Shibpodo said, 'Can you shift a little, Aamodi boudi? Panchi-r ma, help her please? Let me put down a mat here and get Jongol-da out from the room.'

Panchi-r ma said, 'There's an awful stink in there. Jongol pissed and shat all over the place.'

'Everyone shits their guts out when dying,' Shibpodo said confidently. 'The soul doesn't always leave easily. Sometimes it goes out through the mouth, sometimes through the other end. I'll bring him out, I don't care about the smell.'

Aamodi had been wailing in a corner of the yard, where she had flung herself to the ground. It was as much a yard as it was a road; everyone in the slum had equal rights to this space. The inhabitants of the four shacks on the northern side passed through it on their way to and from home. Several people joined hands to bring Jongol out from inside the shack to the yard, and laid him down on a mat spread in the shade of a pair of guava trees that had sprung up on their own.

Bhegai said, 'It doesn't look right for the dead body to be lying here all day. Shall we go get the cot and flowers now?'

The question was meant for Aamodi, but it was Shibpodo who answered: 'Of course. Jongol-da can't be strung up on a bamboo pole like someone run over by a train.'

Moharaj wasn't happy with the way things were going. He shot off a question towards Aamodi. 'Well, Aamodi, something you want to say? Or do you want to give up the body without asking for anything?'

She might have been overwhelmed by her own performance of grief, but Aamodi hadn't lost her common sense. She was quick to catch Moharaj's hint. So she lobbed the ball right back at him. 'What can I say, Mowaraj-da? I'm a mere woman, they say women are half of men. You're my elder brother, you can tell them everything I would, and more. I'm authorising you.'

The young men of the railway slum had staged a performance of *Noti Binodini* some time ago. Aamodi had been to see it, and remembered Girish Ghosh saying the same thing to Ramakrishna Paramhansa.

Moharaj smiled to himself. Aamodi had elevated his status—a fitting reply to Bishnu's slur. His was now the last word in the matter of the late Jongol Poramanik, by virtue of the authority vested in him.

Bishnu was upset. You could bargain with the farmer when buying his harvest directly from him, but there was no such luck if the middleman got in the way, for he would add his commission. And yet there was no option, since Aamodi had authorised Moharaj. So he had no choice but to turn to him. 'All right, what are your terms?'

Clearing his throat, Moharaj said, with the knowledgeable air of a village elder, 'Take Jongol, we're making no claims on him. But we need a cash payment of a thousand and one, and that's my last word.'

The three musketeers exchanged astonished glances. A thousand and one rupees! They had never paid so much for a dead body before. Moharaj had named his price like a cut-throat operator.

'I've been in jail,' Moharaj began. 'It taught me many things I'd never learnt outside. I've met some of the people who trade in bodies, spoken to them too. They're the ones who told me how much a body is sold for. I'm not mentioning any figures. It's none of our business whether you sell a body for five thousand or ten, but Aamodi must get her thousand rupees right now. There are rituals to be observed for ten days. She has to buy rice, fruits, ghee. Then there's the cost of the last rites—the chheradhho. Whether she does it at home or goes to the temple, the last rites will cost three or four hundred. Jongol died *haate-khola-pode-mala*, he was forever scrounging for money, even his arse was bare half the time. You must give her the money so she can pay for all this.'

The three musketeers were looking glum. They were not going to be able to pull it off as easily as they had expected. Just as schools made students clever, jails, too, turned fools into smartasses who had figured out how the underworld operated. Now that Moharaj had come to know, he couldn't be deceived any longer.

After a pause, Bishnu said, 'How can we pay so much? We'll have to spend a lot too. The cot, the incense, the flowers ... We'll need some scent too—can you smell him? Climb down a bit so we can take the body away. Let's settle at five hundred.'

Moharaj was saddled with an enormous responsibility. After some thought, he said, 'Split the difference. That way, both of us can be happy. Neither thousand nor five hundred but seven-fifty. The body isn't available at a lower price. Pay seven-fifty and it's yours. Else, leave it here, and I'll see how to handle it.'

Bhorot, who lived at the far end of the slum and claimed he was a baul, was the one with the most financial resources at his disposal. He sang in trains for alms, and lent out the money he earned at high interest rates. Both his sons had grown up now and had decent incomes of their own. They didn't want their father to be begging for a living anymore. They'd tell him, 'We know you had to do it when we were young, but why now?' But Bhorot was unwilling to wind up his main business. He would say, 'You want me to give up what helped me survive, marry, build a house, bring you two up, just because I've made some money now? Being proud of your riches is the first step to losing them.'

Bhorot's elder son ran a paan-bidi shop near the station. He was also an official of the hawkers' committee, which meant he had two sources of income. He was embarrassed by his father's begging. 'Why do you call it begging,' Bhorot would say. 'I'm like the bee collecting honey. Chaitanya himself did it too. I sing for people, they give me money in return. This is what we bauls do. You can't be a baul if you harbour false pride. Singing washes away all pettiness.'

Now Bhorot was at the scene in the hope that Aamodibala would need money. Even if the young men of the slum agreed to take Jongol's body away for the last rites, they would demand cash for hooch and snacks, and for a meal after their return from the crematorium. Did Aamodi have the money? If not, no problem, Bhorot would lend it to her. He charged ten per cent interest from others—borrow a hundred in the morning, return a hundred and ten the next morning. Delay the repayment, and pay a hundred and twenty-one the next day. But he wouldn't charge Aamodi the same rate; he would settle at seven-and-a-half per cent.

The small businessmen in the slum who sold fish and vegetables used to be captive clients for Bhorot once. But now he had a competitor in the form of Jolodhor, who had a contract for picking up all the dead cattle deposited on the field next to the railway siding. He used to skin them and sell their hide. Jolodhor became flush with cash that one time an epidemic broke out, killing cows and bulls indiscriminately. Some people even claimed he had started it himself, that he had hired people to feed poisoned bananas to cattle. Twenty-two cows had died in one night at Hari Singh's dairy. But it was unlikely to have been Jolodhor, for it needed both courage and political clout to do something like this. People said a private builder with his eye on the land occupied by the dairy set up by Hari Singh, who had come here from Bihar, was behind it. But it was also true that Jolodhor was very wealthy now, and lent money at high rates of interest. He no longer skinned the dead cattle himself; he employed others to do it, who kept half the proceeds. This was the custom nowadays: as soon as low-caste people came into money, they gave up their caste businesses to turn into upper-class gentlemen. Some of them took jobs as cleaners in municipalities and corporations, signing the attendance register and getting other low-caste persons to do the actual work for a pittance, which they paid out of their own higher salary. Jolodhor dressed in white panjabis and paayjamas these days, the attire of the upper-castes. He took up position on a bench at a tea-stall with his bag of money, where many upper-class people borrowed from him, taking and returning their loans furtively to keep their social prestige intact.

Jolodhor's principle was to charge a higher rate for smaller loans but a lower rate for larger ones. So anyone who borrowed less than a thousand rupees had to pay a hundred rupees as interest the next day, but a loan of a thousand meant an interest of only fifty. Jolodhor would say, 'The money won't lay eggs at home; it has to go into other people's houses. The eggs can be large or small, it doesn't matter.'

This was where Bhorot had lost out to Jolodhor. Some of the hawkers and vendors around the station borrowed as much as they needed in the morning, returning their loans with interest at night. Jolodhor applied the same system to them. Which meant the borrowers took a thousand even if they needed less, because they knew the difference between ninety on nine hundred and fifty on a thousand. They had all shifted allegiance from Bhorot to Jolodhor.

Bhorot was apprehensive today. What if Jolodhor beat him to it? So he had arrived at Aamodi's door early with the money tucked in his bag. But now it seemed she wouldn't need the money after all.

The moneylender in Bhorot was deeply distressed. What times were these, when a man became so valuable after his death? Vultures would fight over corpses once upon a time; today, it was human beings.

He would have to leave. There was no point wasting time here trying to net the big fish while the small fry escaped elsewhere. But he wanted to make his presence felt before leaving, he wanted to make a memorable contribution to Jongol Poramanik's life story. So he said, 'You must negotiate, of course. All I have to say is, don't end with a zero, add a one. Make it seven fifty-one.'

Bhegai looked daggers at him. 'Are you done? We don't need a crowd here, give us some air to breathe. Allow us to do our work, never mind the useless talk.'

Moharaj was fully in charge now; an authorisation was not to be taken lightly. He said, 'So what's your final offer? We don't have much time—it's getting hot now. Are you ready to pay seven fifty-one?'

The three musketeers withdrew to the guava tree to discuss the matter in low voices while they smoked. Eventually Bhegai said, 'Let's settle it here, Moharaj-da. Five hundred and one, all right? If not, we'll go now instead of wasting our time.'

Moharaj glanced at Aamodi, whose eyes signalled silent gratitude. So he nodded, 'All right. Hand the cash over.'

'What, right now?'

'Obviously. Cash on delivery.'

Bhegai pleaded, 'Let us take the body first and get some money. Who carries cash around? All of us are *haate-khola-pode-mala*, you know that.'

'Bhorot-da is right here, borrow it from him. We have to make some payments too.'

'I have the money,' said Bhorot.

Now Bhegai sounded stricken. 'Don't you trust us at all, Moharaj-da?'

'What if you disappear?'

'By all the gods, we'll pay you this evening.'

Moharaj was in charge. 'All right, take the body. But don't forget what you promised. He who breaks his word is the son of a bastard. Aamodi had better get her money before sunset.' Now he turned to Aamodi and said solemnly, 'Here, light this twig and give it to your son. Let him do the mukhagni and then let Jongol's body go. Let them take it away, no point keeping it here any longer.'

Going up to Moharaj, Bishnu whispered in his ear that the mukhagni should be done carefully; the ritual of touching the mouth of the corpse with a burning twig had better not leave a scar on the skin. Then he told Gogon, 'Let them do what they have to, we'll wait. You'd better run to Kaalo-da's shop for the flowers, incense and cot. Quick.'

Bhegai added a reminder, 'Don't forget the scent. Jongol-da has shat and pissed all over himself. Who knew what he ate; the smell is too much.'

Aamodi threw an angry glance at them. 'What do you mean who knows what he ate? I cooked fresh fish curry for him last night.'

Gogon sped off towards Kaalo's shop without waiting to hear the rest. The sooner things were done, the better. Delays could lead to unexpected obstacles. When Chandu's wife died, it was obviously a natural death. Gogon and the rest of them had made the arrangements to take the body away. All that was left was to hoist her into the back of the small truck, when the police turned up unexpectedly. But why? A post-mortem was necessary. Someone had complained to the police station that Chandu had beaten his wife to a pulp last night.

That was that, the body never came their way afterwards. And yet they had been so hopeful. She had died barely six hours earlier; the corpse wasn't cold yet. It would have taken an hour and a half to get to their destination, enough time for them to do the things they had to. But the body went to the hospital instead, and Chandu, to jail.

Kaalo's shop was directly opposite KPC Hospital. Earlier, he used to pile the cots meant for corpses on the pavement just outside the entrance. But visitors had objected. The sight of the cots apparently frightened patients so much that they got even sicker. Even those not meant to die ended up dying. Although this meant more business for Kaalo, and better population control, he had been moved to a new location in response to the complaints from patients' families.

Kaalo realised when he saw Gogon run up, gasping for breath, that the fish must have swallowed the bait. Smiling with a display of yellowed teeth, he said, 'How may I serve you, saar?' Though not always, nor with everyone, he did use this formal language with a select few customers. It was not deference, however, but mockery. Kaalo derived satisfaction from ridiculing certain people.

Gogon conveyed his requirements. 'Need a cot, not rickety like last time, make sure it's strong. Plus flowers, incense, a white sheet and some scent.'

'What's the white sheet for?' Kaalo taunted Gogon again. 'It's not your father that's died, is it?'

Gogon said, 'Of course not. It's to cover the body with.'

'Got the cash? Or want it for free?'

'Have we ever paid you in advance? All accounts will be settled in the evening, after we take the body home.'

'Pay a bit now.'

'Honest, Kaalo-da, got no cash.'

'Not even ten? Not even five?'

'Not even enough to buy some poison.'

'Just opened the shop, the first sale can't be made on credit. Go find some cash.'

Gogon pleaded desperately, 'You know very well, Kaalo-da, no one will lend us even a rupee. It's just that you love us ...'

There was a hint of a smile on Kaalo's face in response to Gogon's buttering. 'You people are a pain,' he said, taking a one-rupee coin out of his pocket and handing it to Gogon. 'Hold on to this, and give it to me when you've got all you need. Business was bad yesterday, let's see if you can bring me luck today.'

Pausing, he continued, 'Make sure no one sees you returning the cot. People have become chutiyas these days. If they see, they'll raise hell. I'll smash your balls if that happens.'

Once Gogon was back with all the equipment, three or four of the people who were still there lifted Jongol onto the cot. Aamodi had another bout of crying, but this time one could swear she wasn't putting it on. Jongol had been her companion for seven long years, after all. He would neither abuse her anymore, nor beat her up. Weeping, she hiccupped: 'Take a last look at your father, Giril. You'll never see him again.'

With the three musketeers hoisting three corners of the cot, Shibpodo ran towards the fourth one. 'Bolohori,' screamed Moharaj, and several others echoed the cry that accompanied the dead to their pyres: 'Horibol'. The tranquillity of the morning was replaced by genuine grief now; for some unknown reason, the madman who wandered around with a sack stuffed with scraps of paper began to sob.

Carrying the corpse on their shoulders, they walked a short way along the railway line before lowering it into the shade of the banyan tree beside the ticket counter at the station.

This was the route most of the train passengers preferred on their way to and from work. Bishnu and Gogon took their positions next to the body, the objective being to extract anything between twenty and fifty rupees from every fishmonger or vegetable vendor or liquor supplier who passed. Requests or threats, whatever worked. Many people believed it was good luck to spot a dead body in the morning; the one-, two- and five-rupee coins began to pour in.

A recently constructed temple stood beneath an ancient banyan tree, next to which a row of rickshaws was parked. From Shiva, Kali and Radha to Krishna and Manasa, idols of many deities were present. There was no temple here earlier, there was only the rickshaw line. But the rickshaw-drivers found it impossible to get passengers, the reason being a lethal southern breeze that brought in the kind of smells which made stopping here impossible. Since local trains didn't have lavatories, the passengers who got off at the station used this spot below the tree to relieve themselves.

While the tree received a copious supply of fertilizer, the smell was unbearable.

Very close to the banyan tree was a tea-stall, whose owners had a running feud with the urinating populace on the grounds that their customers were dwindling, and women refused to give them any business. So it was incorrect and inappropriate of them to do what they were doing. As for those dispensing urine, their statement was, 'We believe in tradition. We are merely following in the footsteps of our predecessors who did the same thing here. It is both wrong and unjust to force us to break the tradition.' Sometimes the dispute would turn into fisticuffs.

The controversy might have continued for a long time, when one of the rickshaw-drivers whom the rest considered an imbecile had a brainwave. Without informing anyone, he applied a successful formula to stave off urinating and the resultant stench.

He was on his way back after a trip to Bibek Nogor when he spotted a woman sitting alone in a dark corner of a field. Seized by a vile impulse, he wrapped his arms around her and hoisted her onto his rickshaw. The woman was in fact an idol of the goddess Shitala. Hindu deities had different tastes when it came to being worshipped. Some preferred fresh blood from a goat, and others, fruits. The methods of their disposal after worship were different too. Idols of Durga or Lakshmi or Kali were supposed to be immersed in water, but when it came to Shitala or Manasa, they were meant to be deposited in an open space somewhere.

There was considerable doubt whether worshipping Shitala helped cure small pox or chicken pox, but it had been established that she could be used effectively to strike fear in the hearts of humans. This fear now played an important role in preventing urination here. The rickshaw-driver placed four bricks in the thick mixture of mud and yellow puddles under the banyan tree, and installed the idol on it. Passers-by stopped pissing the very next day, and soon they even started tossing twenty-five- and fifty-paise coins in this direction. A Brahmin in the area realised the spot's potential, built a temple there, and imported idols of as many different gods as possible. There was no knowing who the favourite god of each of those who walked by was, so it was best to have a pantheon on view to remove all obstacles in the way of the coins. The self-appointed priest and his family were now living happily off the takings.

Gogon, Bhegai and Bishnu sighed with envy sometimes. 'If only we had been born into a fucking Baamun family, we'd have been rolling in money by now.'

When they had lain the corpse down, Bhegai, who also drove a rickshaw, said, 'So I'd better be off for Gobordanga now. You two take care of Jongol. The tyre was leaking, so I'd left it at the garage. If they've repaired it, I'll take the rickshaw, else, a bus ...'

'Tell Mohipal-da to take the body away quickly,' said Gogon. 'He'd better not leave it till the night like he did the last time. And tell him to get a bottle of meletaari maal. That rum last time, oho, I can still taste it!'

Bhegai said hesitantly, 'I'm trusting the two of you and leaving the body here. Don't betray me. Make sure the earnings are shared, don't cheat me—I'll be very upset.'

Bishnu grinned. 'Don't worry, we'll save every paisa of your share for you. Better go now, it's getting late.'

Monkhushi, who seemed half-mad, was one of the beggars at the station. She used to be fair-skinned and healthy, but a drunken man had tried to rape her one night. The half-mad Monkhushi had squeezed his testicles so hard that he had almost died. Two other drunks who were waiting for their turn threw themselves at her to save the first one. Monkhushi was injured slightly in the process, bleeding from the nose and mouth. She had saved herself from being raped, though.

But while Monkhushi had succeeded, another mad woman named Ponchomi had not. One or more people had forced her into an empty freight car of a goods train and raped her. She became pregnant as a result, and gave birth to a child at the appropriate time. But though Ponchomi was the mother, it was Monkhushi who had brought the boy up. Ponchomi could barely keep her clothes on; how was she going to manage a child?

Now, Monkhushi came up to Jongol Poramanik's corpse with the child in her arms. 'When you put the body in the cart, give me the sheet, all right?' she told Gogon. 'I'll use it for my son.'

Gogon snapped at her. 'We'll see, get out of here now, let me do my work. Got no money but wants a ticket!'

The unbearable heat was driving everyone crazy in any case, and Monkhushi was halfway there. Silent at first, she screamed in response, 'Just see what I do if you don't give it to me.'

'What will you do, what can you do to me?' Gogon lost his temper as well. 'Tear it off if you dare.'

'Oh really?' Monkhushi was spitting fire now. 'All right, I'll tell everyone who this boy's father is. I know everything. Just because I don't open my mouth, doesn't mean I have no idea. It was your doing, you did it. Fucking drunkard, don't know how to keep your cock in when you're pissed!'

'Stop, stop,' Bishnu moaned. 'Shut up, everyone's listening.'

'Then promise to give me the sheet. I'll go on screaming till you promise.'

'You'll get it, nobody else, I promise.'

Gogon felt as though the corpse in front of him was not Jongol Poramanik's but his own, as though the madwoman Monkhushi had at this very moment throttled him to death and dumped his body in the dust, and everyone—from the rickshaw-drivers to the hawkers and porters—was staring at him.

The dead body would slowly rot and start stinking; white insects would infest it. Anyone who saw it would throw up. Gogon's head began to reel. The very world which had seemed so dazzling a short while ago was now drowning in a sea of tar. He couldn't see a way out of the darkness, though the wheels of the train thundering towards him could rescue him from everything. They only had to roll over his body once for all the fear and anxiety and humiliation to vanish. He gazed at the train roaring in from the distance, without taking his eyes off it.

3

Imaan sauntered towards the bridge that lay ahead. He had seen it many times from the first floor window of the jail. And every time he gazed at the hundreds walking across it, he wished he could be like them and walk beneath the open sky. That day had arrived, so now he was moving about as he pleased, enjoying every step. His eyes glowed with wonder, for he had never imagined walking in the same place as free people, never imagined standing where he could get an unobstructed view of the sky. And so he was savouring the taste of freedom. The bright morning sunlight lit up his face. Buses packed with passengers roared past with blaring horns, leaving a trail of dust. Yellow taxis sped by. A work-obsessed metropolis had started running as soon as it had woken up, with not a glance to spare for those who couldn't keep pace or had slipped and fallen.

Imaan had a government seal on his arm, allowing him to travel without a ticket on buses or trams or trains. He could go as far as he liked—but still he didn't take a bus. He had no address, nowhere to go. This was also one reason to walk. He was dreaming of going somewhere far away. How far? He didn't know.

A filthy, blackened current of water was flowing under the bridge. Some people were using fishing nets attached to hoops to catch small fish in this putrid water. Some were even bathing in it. Imaan had always dunked a plate in a tank of water and poured it on himself; he had never seen anyone actually dipping themselves in water for a bath. He looked on in astonishment. The jail authorities gave every prisoner a plate and a blanket. The plate had to be used for food, bathing and even cleaning oneself after a shit. Imaan had no idea yet that, in the world outside, different utensils were used for food and hygiene. There were many things he didn't know yet. He was like an alien who had only just arrived on this planet. So he greedily took in the scenes around him, and his eyes held wonder at everything he saw.

Just at the foot of the bridge, there was a small shop running out of a kiosk on the right. The shopkeeper had painstakingly laid out a pile of fried chickpeas on an upside-down drum, with dry chillies wedged inside. Next to it was a sack of muri. Someone was frying up reddish luchis and stacking them in a basket, the aroma titillating passers-by. A few poor labourers were standing on the bridge, blowing on the piping hot luchis before biting into them.

Imaan was familiar with luchis—he had tasted them on occasion. Once a year, during Durga Puja, members of the Marwari community sent halwa and luchi to the jail, four luchis per head. Apparently, they weren't fried in oil or Dalda, but in pure ghee.

Imaan was tempted to try a couple of luchis—he would have had his breakfast by now in the jail—but he would have to quell his desires. His friends in jail had said nothing outside was free. Even water for drinking had to be bought at times. All that Imaan had was the generous gift of twenty rupees from the guard at the gate.

A little farther on, he found a temple with an idol of Hanuman smeared with vermilion. Monkeys often visited the trees that stood not far from the jail, jumping between them and breaking the branches. The same monkey was being worshipped here, with a priest ringing a bell and performing the rituals. Some women, none of whom seemed to be Bengali, were standing with plates piled with incense, flowers and other unknown things, waiting to offer them to the idol.

A set of steps behind the temple led down to the foetid creek. There was a row of small brick rooms, and on either side of the steps and below them stood several young women in finery. The occupants of those tiny, confined rooms, they were smiling, talking and nudging one another, exuberant with youth.

Imaan had seen women before, but no more than one or two. When they were taken from the female ward to the court and back, he too would line up with the men and drink them in with thirsty eyes. He had even seen many of the men sighing in frustration over their deprived lives. But those jailed women weren't dressed like this, they didn't giggle; they looked like birds that had weathered a storm. How could anyone laugh when they had a case under the IPC hanging over their heads? This was the first time Imaan was seeing so many women laughing at the same time. He hadn't known women to be capable of laughing, or that their laughter could be so vivacious and unrestrained, so beautiful and lively.

There was a young woman near the bridge, fair, with a round face, a dimple appearing in her cheek every time she laughed. She looked very familiar to Imaan. Had he seen her before? In reality, or in his dreams? He couldn't recollect. She was looking the other way, but now she turned around and caught sight of Imaan's eager, pleading expression, and laughed with joy at once. She seemed pleased, as though she had been waiting for someone just like him all morning. Suddenly, she lifted her right arm, the one with the wrist enclosed in glass bangles, and beckoned to him—come here, you.

Imaan was surprised at this unexpected invitation. She's calling me. Why? I did nothing wrong, I was only looking. Everyone who's passing by is looking. What harm have I done?

Any attempt to talk to a woman in jail would have meant being skinned alive by the guards. The terror of spending all his life in jail still clung to him. He had heard there was a place named Harkata Lane, where the police conducted raids, arresting many young women of this age and bundling them into prison. The new prisoners sometimes met inmates whom they knew earlier. Forgetting where they were, they exchanged smiles and pleasantries. Imaan had witnessed the tragic outcome that befell them. So he stood stock-still, unable to decide whether to advance or retreat.

None of his friends who went in and out of jail were members of cultured society in that sense. They were all wild and reckless, and their lives were rich with diverse experiences. They would tell many stories about women, which he had quite enjoyed listening to. But there was a gulf of difference between listening to stories of tiger hunts and actually being face-to-face with a tiger in the forest. Excitement was transformed into terror.

The woman now climbed up the steps of the bridge, and planted herself in front of Imaan, less than a foot away. A sweet fragrance assailed his senses. Imaan didn't know what it was. Was this how women smelt? Juhi, Chompa, Chameli, Joba—these were women's names, and the names of flowers too. Flowers were supposed to be fragrant. Imaan was familiar with only one kind of flower, which he could see through the window of his ward in jail. One of the trees in the distance, beside the canal, would explode with red flowers at a particular time of the year. The leaves were no longer visible then, hidden behind clumps of these flowers. Polash, someone had said. It's my name, he had added. Normally, it's girls who are named after flowers, but so am I. Which was how Imaan had learnt how this one flower looked, but he hadn't learnt about any of the other flowers in the world.

The young woman had kajol in her eyes and a layer of powder on her face. Her nails were painted red and she had a yellow ribbon in her hair. Her body, like a lissome vine, was wrapped in a sari, a tender shade of green, hiding deep, unknown mysteries. The rise and fall of her breasts with her breathing felt like his death-knell. Imaan was bathed in sweat for some reason; his heart was hammering, his breathing, ragged.

She was bold and animated, not broken with fear like the women he had seen in jail. Without a care for who might be watching or saying something or rushing up with a baton, she came to a halt like an empress in front of Imaan, who was rooted to the spot. The people, the vehicles, even the policeman smoking not far away—all seemed to be under her command, answerable to her. All she had to do was raise a hand for them to kneel at her feet.

With fingers shaped like birds' beaks and ending in painted nails, she took Imaan's hand. Some men were fearful by nature, stopping at the door, lacking the courage to push it open and enter. The woman knew this from experience, which was why she had come up to him and taken his hand. 'Come,' she said. She could feel Imaan's hand trembling in hers. 'You want to, don't you?' she said. 'Don't worry. Come.' Now, it was not just his hand but his entire body that was trembling. He felt the ground beneath his feet shaking. Imaan was melting like wax under her soft, magical touch. His quivering voice held a stricken query: 'Come where?'

A stream of people were walking across the bridge, each of them darting looks like arrows at faces and breasts, thighs and hips. A long procession of cars and buses kept moving. The city at rush hour. Who was it who had just whispered in his ear like music amidst this cacophony, 'Want to? Come.'

A temple stood almost directly beneath the bridge, the branches of a peepul tree bending over its tip. Birds were cooing on its branches, while its green leaves rustled in the breeze, and the sunlight glinted on their surface. But who had spoken?

The woman's soft fingers were still holding Imaan's captive. As though they were trying to elicit his consent with their touch. Again, Imaan asked in desperation, 'Come where?'

'To my room. You want to, don't you? Come.'

Was it an invitation or an order? Imaan wasn't sure. He wasn't sure why or what was involved. This was not an aspect of life he knew of. He had stepped into a new world just a few minutes ago, he needed some time to adjust to this light, this air. And so, he asked in astonishment, 'Why?'

It was the woman's turn to be surprised. What kind of boy had she found herself with? He was lapping up her body a moment ago; it was obvious what was on his mind. And now that I'm giving you the chance to fulfil your desire, you're saying, 'Why?' Are you really a fool, or only pretending to be one? Like an angry snake, she hissed, 'I told you. So you can do what you want to do. You want to, don't you?'

Imaan didn't know what he wanted to say when he shook his head. It meant 'no'. She was offended. 'You don't think I'm pretty? You don't like me?'

Imaan felt something eluding him. Life hadn't taught him the right responses, or the hidden meaning of words.

It was an invitation, not an attack, but Imaan felt that the alluring look in those eyes and the seductive smile were wrapping themselves around him like a python. He was trapped. The men in jail had said a woman was like a river—deep, beautiful, wild, cooling, all of those at once. But to someone who didn't know how to swim, a river was the goddess of death. Which was why Imaan shook his head to say no. You are gorgeous, but my heart cannot respond to your call. I'm terrified, my heart is quaking. I cannot go with you. Forgive me for not accepting your hospitality. Imaan wanted to run away as far as possible.

Not that he said any of this. He only shook his head and took a small step backward. But the young woman blocked his way, her eyes blazing, her voice breathing fire. 'How dare you shake your head! Am I not pretty? Am I ugly?'

Imaan was speechless.

She jerked angrily at his hand, which was still held in hers. 'Well? Am I pretty or not?'

Imaan seemed to come to his senses. Startled, he said, 'Oh yes, you're pretty, you're very pretty.'

'What's wrong then?'

'Wrong?'

'Why won't you come with me?'

Unable to understand why a woman wanted to take a complete stranger into her home, Imaan asked, 'But why should I come with you? For what?'

Now she flew into a temper. 'Are you pretending to be innocent? Don't you know what's what? Why do men come here? Why do they come into our houses? You don't know? Are you here first thing in the morning to pray? Don't act smart with me, I'll take everything you have and kick you out. If you know what's good for you, just follow me quickly. First trade of the day—don't make me angry. Ask anyone, they'll tell you how well I treat them if they're good. But to the devil, I'm an even bigger devil.' She was snorting in rage now.

At last, there was a glimmer of light in the darkness. Imaan was beginning to grasp the situation. So she was one of them. His friends had told him many stories about them—not all good, but not all bad, either. They were supposed to be generous, they gave you everything. Everything. But they charged for it too. Bijoy had warned him, though. 'Never trust them. From their hair to their toenails, everything about them is a lie. You'll never win their hearts—not even with a million bucks. You'll get love only as long as you have money; they'll hold you close and say the sweetest things. The day you can't pay, they'll kick you out. They have no hearts, they're just dolled-up machines. Like machines they smile, they weep, they win you over with practised lines. And when they realise you have nothing more to give them, they'll slam the door in your face and go to bed with someone else. Money is all they know, money.'

But then Ananto had said just the opposite. 'People call them whores—this is wrong. They're humans too, just like us. They have hearts, they cry when they're hurt, they laugh when they're happy. They, too, want to love someone deeply; they want to get love too. I'd actually say no one can love the way whores—okay, everyone calls them that so I'm using the same word—can. If they love you, you've got everything on earth. They can happily die for you. I'm not making this up. Dying is no big deal for them. They get money, clothes, but never love. All the men who talk to them of love are liars; they only want their bodies. And when they're done with one of them, they run off to another one.'

Here were two people, both telling the truth. But how could there be two truths?

Imaan could feel the young woman's grip on his hand tightening, like the noose of manila rope around the neck of a convict. She was pulling him along. He was being forced to go with her. The steep staircase loomed in front of him, going all the way down to a cave in the middle of hellfire. The women leaning against the railings on both sides were giggling at Imaan's discomfiture.

It was morning. Morning, for all intents and purposes. Certainly for those who went to sleep very late at night. Many of the women hadn't woken up yet. Those who were awake had bathed, washed off last night's dirt and filth, cleansed themselves, combed their hair and put fragrant flowers in it, and were standing outside their rooms for sunlight, fresh air, and, who knew, maybe some money in case there was a customer.

But whether there was a customer or not, there was no choice but to go outside. How long could anyone stay cooped up in these pigeonholes? Brick walls with tile roofs, about two dozen cubicles in all, each occupied by one woman. All of them lived as tenants. And here the rent was calculated not monthly but on a daily basis. The owner didn't live here. The woman who collected rent on his behalf was referred to as Baariuli ma by everyone. You could have had a full meal or you could be starving, but the rent had to be paid to her every morning. She was very strict about this, refusing to take no for an answer. She had been abused many times, and given as good as she'd got. But no invective enraged her as much as the words 'can't pay the rent today'. Her response to this was impossible to gauge. She had a lot to manage—the police, local hoodlums, party leaders. Sometimes there were even court cases, which needed a lawyer. When the rent wasn't paid, she'd storm into the room and throw the occupant's possessions out on the street, screaming, 'See if you can find another place as peaceful as this one, you bitches. Who's going to protect you from the police and the hoodlums and the leaders like I do? I look after the lot of you like a mother would. Why do I do it? You have to protect your assets, that's why. But if you don't pay the rent, am I supposed to sell my own body to pay for everything?'

The lane ran past the stairs on both sides, with a peepul tree on its left. On the right, it went all the way to the edge of the creek, and on the left, to the main road. Up ahead of the bridge was an L-shaped intersection where the lane hit the populous street, which ran from west to east, at a right angle. There was a crowd of women at both ends of the lane now, some standing, some sitting. Some milled about aimlessly, some drank tea from earthen cups. Some were racing off now and then to stir the pot of rice on the stove.

This was a slow time for business, which picked up only as evening approached. And when it was dark, the respectable men from genteel society would appear, taking care not to allow their reputations to be besmirched. The darkness knew how to conceal their bhodrolok identities.

But those who had no reputation to maintain could visit even in the morning or afternoon. The customer was God, he could never be spurned.

The day was split into two halves: morning and evening. Anyone who could entertain what was called a chhoot babu or bhokatta ghuri—a solitary, casual customer—was able to get an early start on reaching her targeted income for the day. These casual customers had no fixed women whom they patronised; they went in with whoever was available. Not everyone had regular customers—the bandha babus who guaranteed a regular income—so these chhoot babus were one way to compensate.

The competitive shouting for customers, like for bus passengers or buyers at the market, erupted in the evening.

Right now, everyone was in a state of languorous indolence. Customers were welcome, but the women weren't going to take the initiative.

One babu meant rent, two meant groceries, three meant clothes and medicines and finery, four meant some savings. Everyone wanted to have this line-up of four somehow, and the rest was a bonus.

The young woman was grumbling now as they marched on. 'Everyone's clever and we're the fools, right? If you're passing this way, just walk on, who's stopping you? But you'll stand on the bridge and gape at us for hours—why? Is this a free movie? Are our bodies available free of cost? Makes me furious, makes me want to drown them in this rotting creek.'

'Can I say something?' Imaan asked in trepidation.

'As many things as you like.'

'What's your name?'

'Why do you want to know? You want to complain? You want to go to the police station?'

'Of course not, why should I complain?'

'Then what do you want to know my name for? Do your job and get out.'

'You're very beautiful. I thought your name must be beautiful too. That's why I'm asking.'

'My name?' She frowned at Imaan. 'I wonder what my name is. Oh, I remember, it's Aishwarya. You know the heroine? I'm named after her. Do you like the name? Apparently I look a lot like her—that's what everyone says. Is it true?'

'How would I know? I've never seen her.'

'You don't watch movies?'

'I've heard of them. Never seen any.'

The boy didn't watch movies. Aishwarya wasn't surprised, but she didn't feel bad for him either. Why spend so much money on tickets? Those who stared at women in flesh and blood might not be fascinated by films.

She was about to speak when someone behind them called out harshly: 'Can the discussion be moved to the side? How will people walk if the road is blocked?' It was a familiar face, whose owner patronised a woman named Rasha. No matter which time of day he appeared, he arrived like a whirlwind and left like one too.

The lane was extremely narrow, no more than four- or five-feet wide. The rooms faced one another across it. Taking a bunch of keys tucked into her sari at the waist, Aishwarya unlocked her door. Inside, there was a cot, with only a little space left over to walk around. The cot stood on bricks, allowing enough space beneath it for her cooking utensils to be stored. She had very few of them—just a few pots and pans to cook for one or, at most, two, on a kerosene stove in the tiny space left free on the floor. She hadn't started cooking yet today.

A rope was slung between two nails in the walls, on which hung a small number of saris, petticoats, brassieres and gamchhas. On another wall was an image of the goddess Kali, with an ancient garland of plastic hibiscuses hung around it. The goddess had a red tongue and blazing eyes.

Aishwarya locked her door on entering, switched on the fan, took off her sari, and hung it lightly on the rope. Squatting, she laid out a rush mat on the floor, and put a pillow at the head. Arrangements for the guest to lie down. Customers were not allowed to use the bed, only the mat could be soiled.

Imaan could see a great deal more of her now. His eyes were smarting, his heart was thumping, his throat was dry.

'Some water.'

'You'll get it. Water and anything else you want. Get the cash out first. Once I've got my money, I'll give you all you want.'

All Imaan had was that one red twenty-rupee note the guard had given him. It wasn't so much money as it was a lifeline. If it slipped out of his hands, he'd be left with nothing. A long day of starvation lay ahead. Who was going to feed him without payment?

Imaan had left the safe haven he had enjoyed all these years to enter the world of free people. No one would take care of him here; he alone would be responsible for his own survival—or death. Who knew what unknown dangers lay ahead? And so, he was wracked by doubt about whether to part with the only money he had. Eventually, he told himself, we'll worry about the future later, let's see what happens now; let me extricate myself from this peril first. With tired, trembling fingers, he held out the red twenty-rupee note to the woman.

'Here you are.'

'What!' She looked incredulous. 'Just twenty!'

'I don't have any more. I'm giving you all I have.'

'Are you joking with me? You've come to a whorehouse with twenty bucks! Take off your shirt, we know the likes of you only too well. We know where you hide your money.'

In jail, only those who had completed their sentence got proper clothes. Those under trial had to get their own from outside. Imaan was somewhere in between, so he had two kinds of attire—a shirt from outside, pants issued by the jail. Sometime earlier, a convict who was under trial had passed on an extra shirt to him after getting bail. A ward mate named Hardayal had given him the pants. Since prisoners got two new pairs every year, they gave away the old ones. Imaan's pants were handloom ones, white in colour. And the shirt, terry cotton, dark blue. He took his shirt off without demur and handed it over to the woman. She searched through the pocket, the underarm, the collar and the hems thoroughly. This was how new convicts were frisked in jail to check for money, weed, or blades. 'Take your pants off,' Aishwarya demanded when she was done with the shirt. 'There's nothing underneath,' Imaan croaked in panic.

'Nothing?' Her eyes flashed. 'Are you impotent?'

'No, I mean, I have no underwear.'

She handed him a gamchha. 'Use this and take them off.'

'This is torn.'

'Who cares? Who besides me is seeing anyway? Everyone here shows me everything they have; they come here to see everything too. Are you telling me you don't know? I'm going to lose my temper now. This is time for business—the whole day will go to hell if I waste time. Take them off quick!'

There was no choice. Imaan was terrified by her aggression. She combed through the pants too, but there was nothing. She was surprised—had the fool really come here with just twenty rupees? It wouldn't even buy him a kiss. Did he have no idea how he would be humiliated now? All she had to do was call out to one of the goons outside to have him beaten up. They'd keep his clothes and kick him out wrapped in newspapers. Was he new to this then? With no experience at all?

'Have you been here before? To any of the girls' rooms?'

'No, first time.'

Now she examined Imaan carefully. A newly sprouted moustache and beard, as yet unshaven. A childlike simplicity in his eyes. Fear and hesitation written all over him.

She said, 'Didn't anyone tell you you need lots of money to come here?'

'They did. Those who've been here said it costs a lot.'

'Then why did you turn up with empty pockets?'

'I didn't want to. You forced me. I wouldn't have otherwise. I was only passing by—I looked at you because you're so beautiful. You grabbed me.'

'*Ki mithyuk re baba!* How you can lie! You're so beautiful—you know all the lines, don't you? No one will be able to tell looking at you, but such a Romeo. You think I'm the only beautiful woman on earth? You can see so many women, far more beautiful than me, wandering about on the streets.'

Was he actually a smartass in disguise then? Maybe he had taken a chance to see if he could have some fun without paying for it and was flattering her so he could escape. Now she was spewing poison. 'Never seen anyone like me? Anyone who? Another woman, or another hooker?'

'What's a hooker?'

'A woman, for fuck's sake. Never seen a woman before?'

'Believe me, I really haven't.' Imaan realised he'd made a mistake as soon as he said it. He continued, trying to correct himself, 'No, I've seen women. When they walked past our ward. And when they walked down the road, if we tried, we could see from our window. The windows were very high; you could only look through them if someone let you climb on their shoulders. But none of them was as beautiful as you. I don't remember seeing anyone so pretty. What a lovely smile you have. I've never spoken like this before; I could never imagine a woman talking to me.'

'Why're you bullshitting me? You're old enough, how could you not have spoken to a woman? Don't you know women also wish for men, just like men wish for women? You really haven't met anyone or spoken to anyone?'

'How would I? No one came as close as you did. No one took my hand either. They didn't allow any of this there. They'd beat us up if we tried.'

The young woman was bewildered. Was it true what he was saying? In these liberal times, when all kinds of things took place between men and women, a boy of twenty or so was claiming he had never even spoken to a girl, he had never seen a beautiful woman. She could still accept the second, for tastes varied from one person to the next. But never even talked to a woman? Which planet had he descended from? And yet, for some reason, he made her feel he wasn't lying. He was certainly an adult, as his moustache and beard and the hair on his chest showed, but his entire body was enveloped in an adolescent innocence, which even adolescents didn't possess nowadays. It was his unthreatening appearance that had given her the courage to grab his hand. She would never have been able to do it had he looked rough and tough.

These things were necessary in this line of work. There were plenty of men who hung around the area, dying to enter but not daring to. The very thought of going up to one of the women and asking made their hearts thump and their tongues curl up. So the women had to read the signs and take the initiative, sometimes using a little force to dispel their fear, even if this meant grabbing them by the collar and dragging them up to their doors.

Which was what she had done. But now she was dying to know what this boy's name was, where he lived, what he did for a living, and why life had dealt him such a hand of deception.

Imaan was still standing. She made him sit on her cot. He had asked for some water; she poured him a glass. Then she started speaking, calmly. 'Where did you come from? Where were you going?'

Pointing to the south, Imaan said, 'That's where I came from.' The young woman smiled and pointed to the north. 'And is that where you were going?'

'I wasn't going anywhere,' he answered candidly. 'I don't know any place in this city. So I was just standing there wondering where to go.'

'You don't know where you're going?'

'I don't.'

'And you don't know any place you'd like to go to?'

'No.'

Was he mad? An imbecile? Or cunning? He spoke in riddles. Her voice tinged with irritation, she said, 'You don't know any place in Calcutta, in Bengal, in India, in the world? You have nowhere to go?'

'That's right.'

'Fine. What about where you came from? Does it have a name? Do you know it?'

'I do. It's called Central Jail. That's where I'm coming from.'

Jail! The sunshine in her heart was replaced at once by clouds. The tenderness she was beginning to feel for him shrivelled suddenly. She couldn't make up her mind about what to do. Entertain him, or throw him out? She was torn between wanting to make him a cup of tea and slapping him for spoiling her morning business opportunity. By turns he seemed simple and sly, foolish and evil. He had come from the jail, he had said. What was he trying to tell her? I'm a seasoned criminal—give me what I want without payment. Was he trying to intimidate her? Or was he giving her an honest explanation for being penniless?

Looking him in the eye to show she wasn't afraid, the young woman said, 'So you've been released from Central Jail. You don't know any place outside it, so you don't know where to go. Did you fall into the jail from the sky?'

His friends in jail had told him repeatedly when he was leaving, 'Don't tell anyone you were in prison. You know for yourself how many people have to do time unjustly. People outside don't believe that—they think anyone who's been in jail is a bad person. If they come to know you were here, they will suspect you of being a criminal. Instead of getting help, you'll only get into trouble. If there's a theft or burglary somewhere, they'll catch you and beat you up. Don't tell anyone.'

Imaan hadn't remembered that advice and blurted out the truth. But now he felt this woman wasn't harmful; he could perhaps trust her and give her an account of his vexed life. He would have to tell someone, after all. No one could get by without help from someone else. This was as true outside jail as it was inside. He had nobody to call his own out here. He was, in fact, meeting someone for the first time, someone who could turn out to be good or bad; he didn't know yet. But who could tell she wouldn't turn out to be his closest friend, his greatest treasure?

'No one falls from the sky,' said Imaan, 'they're born. When I was a baby, my mother went to jail. She died there. There was no one to take me away. So I had to stay there all these years. I've finally been set free.'

The sense of mutual cooperation among the women was strong here. There were customers who would refuse to leave, as though trying to extract the highest return on their investment. So everyone knew to knock on any door that remained closed for more than half an hour. Could anyone afford to spend the entire night with a single customer? Not unless they paid for four, which they wouldn't.

Now, one of the women did just this on seeing Aishwarya's door closed for a long time. 'Open the door, you floozy,' she said from outside. 'Someone's looking for you. He's been waiting a long time.'

If she still didn't open the door, the woman would say sternly after a while, 'Open the door, slut. There's going to be a raid—they sent word from the police station. Send your man home.'

But a second rap on the door was not needed, for Aishwarya opened the door at the first knock. Dressed in just a petticoat and blouse, she didn't show herself but only poked her head out. There were seven or eight others like her, sitting on stools at the southern end of the lane. Addressing one of them, she shouted, *'Ei Bondona, Botuk-da ke bol duto boro cha are duto pojapoti bishkoot pathiye dite.'* She shut the door again.

A tiny room, a man and a woman sitting face to face, one of them holding the other's hands in her own. No words. The silence inside was in sharp contrast to the loud noises outside. Bondona shouted back from the end of the lane. 'An hour with the customer and now tea and biscuits too. What's going on? Fallen in love? Don't run away with him now.' Waves of laughter rippled through the lane.

But Aishwarya wasn't laughing. She was weeping for this young man whose story she had just heard. Many such young men came to her. Some of them even put garlands of currency notes round her neck, but her heart never bled for them. Imaan was destitute, a rejected member of society. He had nothing, and yet he had something which made you sad, which made you want to love him.

Sometime later, Imaan said, 'You know my story, now tell me yours.' After a pause, the young woman said, 'I'll tell you. I'll tell you everything, but not today.' Unable to bear the weight of her past, she leaned her head on Imaan's shoulder. Pointing to the wall on the south, she said, 'Do you know the name of the creek there? It's the Ganga, you know. With high tides and low tides. There's a full moon in the sky at the time of the highest tide—you can see its reflection in the water. There will blow a light breeze from the south. Come quietly late on such a night and knock on my door, and I'll tell you everything.'

After another pause, she continued, 'I'll tell you the things I've never told anyone. Never found anyone to tell them to. I have many things in my heart I want to tell, but there's been no one who would listen.'

There was a shelf on the wall to the south, with a few torn, dirty books on it. Imaan didn't know how to read, or he would have found out what the books were about. But he did realise that the woman was educated. Those who were educated spoke in the language of books. Like Shiddhartho, the college student Imaan had met in jail. Imaan didn't understand the things Shiddhartho would say, and he didn't understand what this woman was saying either. He could make some sense of the invitation to visit her at night, but what did the high tide, the full moon, or the southern breeze have to do with all of this? How could so many things come together at the same time?

The tea was here. It was made in advance, and only had to be poured into cups and glasses. Everything hereabouts was off-the-shelf, available instantly for cash—no credit, even if this meant the end of the relationship. Come back for more if you like. If you prefer the shop next door, that's fine too. There will be other customers.

'Drink your tea.'

Imaan burnt his tongue at the very first sip. He had tasted tea before, but it hadn't been piping hot. Was tea always like this in the world outside?

'Will you come again?' The young woman's question was more to herself than to Imaan.

Would he? Would he find his way back here? Her heart was telling her he wouldn't. But she, a woman in prostitution, for whom the company of the male body was anything but rare, could sense a turmoil in her breast that had nothing to do with sex.

'Come again, come at least once more if you can,' she said with feeling. 'I'll wait.'

Finishing his tea, Imaan put his cup down. He could have thrown it away if it was an earthen one, but the shopkeeper would wash it and re-use it. This would go on for months and years—there was no respite for the cup till it broke.

Outside, Bondona was shouting again. 'Open the door, Aishwarya, someone's looking for you.'

'All right,' the young woman replied.

'No, it isn't all right, come see for yourself,' Bondona shouted.

Opening the door a crack like the last time, she poked her head out to discover Bondona wasn't crying wolf. There was indeed someone at the end of the lane, buying cigarettes. An old customer, back after a long time. A clerk at the court. The last time he had said, 'It'll be some time before I'm here next. My youngest daughter is getting married. The boy lives in Madurai. I can't come till all the ceremonies are done.'

'Tell him to come back in a few minutes, tell him there's someone in my room,' Aishwarya said. Turning around, she told Imaan, 'Get dressed and wait on the bridge. I'll be there in half an hour. First trade of the day—can't turn him down. Don't be angry. I'll be with you as soon as I'm done.'

Imaan went out, choked by an unfamiliar pain in his throat. The man went in, leaving his slippers outside, as soon as Imaan left. The door was closed. A sigh. Tears in his eyes.

The sun was blazing down now, turning the earth into a bed of fire. Imaan was barefoot. He had got a shirt and a gamchha as gifts from jail inmates, but no shoes or slippers.

Very few people used the bridge. The bhodrolok avoided this pavement, using the one across the road. And those who picked this one made it a point to ogle at the women, imagining the pleasures of fucking them, perhaps sighing at their own deprived lives compared to the man's who had just left one of the rooms and was climbing up to the bridge.

Imaan didn't feel like waiting. After a last look from the bridge at the narrow lane, he sighed once more and began walking. Rivulets of sweat ran down his body, streaming across the government seal on his arm, all but obliterating it. Imaan wasted no time, jumping into a bus waiting at the bus-stop.

It wasn't particularly crowded, with most of the passengers having found seats, and only a few standing. The bus was ambling along, seemingly moving only because it had to, much against its will. After going north for some time, it turned to the east, and then back to the north after fifteen minutes, continuing at a snail's pace. None of the passengers was in a hurry; some of them were, in fact, fast asleep. Suddenly, Imaan spotted the man who had snarled at him and Aishwarya for blocking the road. He had obviously completed a speed job and had got on the same bus at the earlier bus-stop.

He had spotted Imaan too. Sidling up to him, the man whispered, 'New to this game?' He was leering. 'I knew it was your first time. So how did it go? Did you get it right?'

Imaan couldn't reply—he had no wish to. He only stared at the man, who had a toothbrush moustache and looked like a pig doused in oil, with large imbecilic eyes and lines of sweat-soaked powder in the creases on his neck.

After a pause, he said, 'Don't be embarrassed. There's nothing to be ashamed of. Everyone is inexperienced at first. I was too. My first time didn't go well; the whore was half dead. You, however, picked a sex-bomb. I was a fool. It's dark there near the steps in the evening, so I didn't see her face properly. And the sluts have a no-poaching rule. Or I could have tasted that Aishwarya once, at least. So sexy!'

Imaan had heard such things said in the past too, but he had felt no sadness or rage then. Listening to this man now was making him angry. His tongue was as filthy as he was ugly. And he was talking this way to someone at least twenty years younger.

'Can't change the menu here,' the man continued, 'so I'm thinking of changing the table. Sonagachhi would have been perfect. They have at least twenty thousand women there.' He sounded regretful now. 'But it's too far. I don't have enough time. Here it's a quickie: half an hour to get here, half an hour's stay, half an hour to get back. All done in an hour and a half. My wife's a complete bitch. She doesn't allow me out of the house at all, always checks on where I'm going. The neighbours have poisoned her ears—I have no peace at home. You haven't married yet—good move. Have as much fun as you can before you do. Once you're tied to the pole, there's no escape. Anyway, when are you going there next?'

When was he going there next? Was he going ever? Would he meet the young woman again? Would she hold his hands once more? Who could tell? It wasn't as easy to go back as it was to go away.

The man's presence was intolerable. But Imaan didn't have to take it much longer, for he got off the bus a little later, but not before asking again, 'When are you going there next?' Imaan shook his head. He didn't know.

Imaan didn't know. He had no idea what life was going to bring him even an hour later. He would have to let himself go on the current. The future alone would show where he would wash up ashore. Right now, there was nothing to do but to surrender himself to it.

'Ticket?' A hairy, perspiring arm darted towards Imaan. 'Where's your ticket?' Imaan had never been on a bus or a train, never bought a ticket in his life. But he knew what he had to say now—his friends in jail had taught him. 'You're a government official all day today,' the deputy jailer had joked. 'All you need to do is show the seal on your arm.'

That was what he did now, holding up his arm and saying, 'I don't need a ticket.'

'Don't need a ticket? Do you have a pass? Show me.'

'I have this seal.'

'Seal? What seal?'

'See for yourself.'

Imaan's seal had almost been washed away by sweat, so the conductor asked, 'Tell me what seal this is. Speak up.'

'I was in jail,' said Imaan. 'Got out today. They put this seal on my arm at the gate. Said, I won't need a ticket all day today.'

'What! You were in jail!' The conductor's scream woke the dozing passengers up. Everyone stared at Imaan suspiciously, as though he was an escaped convict, a criminal, a murderer.

'Why were you in jail?' the conductor asked.

'No reason.'

'Not for theft or robbery or rape or murder? Nothing?'

'Nothing,' said Imaan, dispassionately.

'I see.' The conductor was dripping sarcasm. 'But the thing is, this is a private bus, the seal doesn't work here. Buy a ticket, or get off.'

Imaan remembered the twenty rupees he had given the young woman, which she hadn't returned. Perhaps she'd forgotten. Imaan hadn't asked for it either; he'd forgotten too. Maybe she'd have given it back if he'd waited half an hour as she had asked him to. Now his pockets were empty. 'I have no money,' he said.

'Get off then. Take a government bus, your seal will work there.'

One of the passengers sitting by the window was sweating and sleeping. He had come to the city for a court case, and was on his way back now to his village. Woken up by the uproar, he looked at Imaan. For some reason, he felt a wave of sympathy. 'Never mind, let him be,' he told the conductor. 'Everyone else is buying a ticket. If someone has no money, let him be.'

'You want him to travel without paying the fare?'

'Does every passenger buy a ticket? Do you manage to get everyone to pay?'

'I do. No one can escape my eyes. I have four of them, two in front, two at the back.'

'He's not trying to escape your eyes. He's telling you he has no money.' Everyone was staring at them now. 'Would he have shown you that seal if he had any money? He'd have quietly bought a ticket. Leave him alone.'

'He was in jail!'

'He admitted it himself.'

'I'd have let him go if he was honest. I let honest people go. Why should I let a criminal go?'

'How do you know he's a criminal? Who told you everyone who goes to jail is a criminal?'

The conductor couldn't keep his head in the unbearable heat. 'Talk is cheap. I won't let him travel free on my bus,' he said sharply. 'If your heart's bleeding for him, put your money where your mouth is. Everyone's sympathetic till they have to pay up. Buy him his ticket if you can.'

The echo went round the bus. 'Buy him a ticket.'

The man was trapped. He had no choice but to pull out his wallet. Holding out a ten-rupee note, he said, 'Give him a ticket. Don't you dare shout at me, I don't ask anyone to do what I wouldn't.'

'Where are you going?' the conductor asked Imaan rudely.

Where am I going? Imaan was in a quandary. Where do I want to go? He remembered his friend Komol from jail, who had said he was from Mohonpur. You had to get there by train. The train left from a place called the station. You had to get to the station by bus.

'I'm going to the station,' said Imaan, 'where the train leaves from.'

'Yes, I know the train leaves from the station. Which station?'

'The one where the train for Mohonpur leaves from.'

'How should I know?' The conductor was furious. Looking murderously at Imaan's benefactor, he said, 'Please tell me which station the train for Mohonpur leaves from.'

Someone said, 'From Sealdah, as far as I remember.'

'What to do now?' said the conductor. 'This bus doesn't go to Sealdah.'

'Give him a ticket to Jadavpur,' someone else suggested. 'He can take a train to Sealdah from there. He's confused by all the time he spent in jail, so he's taken the wrong bus.'

Everyone was looking at Imaan, without a trace of sympathy. Why should they feel pity for a convict who had done time? The man who had paid for his ticket under pressure had closed his eyes again. He wasn't paying attention anymore. Maybe he was regretting spending the money. Imaan stood guiltily in a corner. The bus kept moving.

After about forty minutes, it stopped halfway up a bridge. Two railway tracks stretched in either direction below it. The up line and the down line. One of them ran straight as an arrow towards the heart of the city, and the other went beyond the villages, towards the distant horizon.

'Get down,' the conductor told Imaan. 'This is Jadavpur Station.'

A number of people were walking down the stairs from the middle of the bridge. Imaan followed them.

4

Polashi felt like her entire body was burning. She arranged the end of her sari over her head in a cowl to protect herself from the sun, which was directly overhead now. Balancing the heavy sack on her shoulders, she tried to speed up to get there quicker. She still had some way to go—at least a mile. Polashi had to walk thirteen or fourteen miles every day. It wasn't so difficult when she began. But the more she progressed, adding to the weight of the sack with things she had picked up on the road, the harder it got, making this last mile almost impossible. She had to get to One-Armed Paanu's scrapyard near the level crossing in Palpara.

Polashi was twenty-four or twenty-five, of healthy build, as tall as the average Bengali woman, but a little on the fairer side. Her skin was covered in a layer of grime now, however. Her nails had not been clipped in a long time, and were filthy as a result. There was dirt in the creases on her neck, too, and her hair had turned brown. Her unwashed blouse was smelling. Still, there was something about her that attracted hungry looks. Maybe it was her breasts, or long nose, or thick lips, or big black eyes. Or all of them.

Walking down East Road, she passed Niloy Nibash and stopped at the banyan tree outside the Mahadeb temple next to the lake, where the shade enticed her into taking a short rest. Lowering her sack to the ground, she sat on it, and at once waves of exhaustion washed over her. She felt drowsy.

The lake stretched a long way, about seven or eight hundred feet from east to west. At the eastern end there was a row of rickshaws, a kiosk selling tea, and another one selling chhatu. Another ragpicker, just like Polashi, was sitting outside the shop, drinking ghol made with chhatu. Many believed this ghol of hot chickpea chhatu was most useful, taking care of both hunger and thirst.

The road next to the lake ran absolutely straight. At other times, it was chock-a-block with cars, taxis and buses, but at the moment there were relatively few vehicles and pedestrians. The place was practically deserted under the afternoon sun, which allowed the young man with the glass of chhatu ghol to spot Polashi sitting at the other end of the lake with her sack. Actually, he had kept his eyes peeled for her. Draining his glass, he paid up quickly and began to march towards the banyan tree, which offered more than just shade.

There was something very heavy in the young man's sack, forcing him to bend over like a geriatric with a walking stick. He dumped the sack on the ground in front of Polashi, whose drowsiness was dispelled at once by a ringing sound. With a smile, she asked, 'What have you got in there, Beji? Sounds like something solid.'

Returning her smile with his yellowing teeth, Beji aka Brojo said, 'You know they're building flats by the boys' club? Fucking labourers have been hiding them in the trees. Small lengths of iron rods. Wanted to sell them once they'd collected enough. Saw them when I went for a shit. I was just waiting for a chance. They went to eat, and I grabbed them.'

Beji laughed loudly. 'Stole from thieves. Twenty-five kilos at least. Fucked my ass carrying them.'

'They'd have skinned you alive if they'd caught you,' Polashi said. 'Those club boys are bastards. They beat up Laden so bad he couldn't get out of bed for a week, couldn't walk for a month.'

His face suffused with the smile of success, Beji said, 'Didn't catch me. Got away. No need to think of ifs and buts.'

After a pause, he continued with a philosophical air. 'Got to take chances. Can't hold back for fear.' Wiping his face with his dirty gamchha, he plonked himself on his sack and carried on. 'Been doing the rounds since morning. Been everywhere, but nothing worthwhile anywhere. Scrubbed fucking clean. Looks like the Bondel gang got there before me. Not their territory. Going to fuck their happiness one of these days. Day was going to hell. Might have had to go home empty-handed and starve. Lucky I got the rods. Will get at least two hundred for them. Food sorted for a few days. Need to take risks these days to survive.'

Wiping the sweat off his forehead again, he grinned. 'What about you, Polashi di?'

Polashi didn't smile back. The look in her eyes was a mix of the familiar and the unfamiliar. 'Am I your sister? When did your father's dick give birth to me? Was I born from your mother's cunt? How the fuck can you call me didi? How old would I have to be to be your elder sister? You think I'm so old?'

Beji looked apologetic. 'Didn't think of all that. Just said it naturally.'

Polashi continued to fume. 'I didn't grow up without food like you. I'm healthy because I ate well. Wouldn't have looked so old if I'd been skinny. I used to work for a Marwari family. They never ate anything but pure milk and butter and ghee. Fifteen kilos of fresh milk every day. They had a machine. If you dipped it in the milk, it told you if any water had been added to it, and how much. You've never seen rutis like theirs. Fat, and dripping with ghee.'

He'd made a mistake. He'd hurt Polashi without meaning to. Now Beji was upset because Polashi was. Driven by the desire to correct his error, he said, 'Didn't mean it. Was trying to get you angry. I like it when you're angry—your face gets so red. I swear, you look so goddamn beautiful then. Believe me, not making it up. I can swear on anyone you want me to.'

Even the gods are pleased by flattery, and Polashi was a mere mortal. The heat went out of her voice. 'Enough, no need to swear. Didn't you swear to take me to Gazi Baba's shrine at Monjilpur? You broke the promise.'

'So now you're blaming *me*. Waited at the station all morning. No sign of you. Kamini said Polashi went somewhere yesterday. Hasn't come back, hasn't told me anything. How is it my fault?'

'I was busy that day. But the day after? And the day after that? Thirty days to a month. You had no time.'

'Did you ask?'

'Why should I? You should have asked. We couldn't go the other day, Polashi. Let's go today.'

'So now it's all my fault. You wanted to go, you fixed the date, and then you didn't go. Now it's your turn to tell me when you want to go, not mine.'

Beji had been bitterly disappointed that day. He had gone to the station with so much hope in his heart, dressed in a laundered shirt, his hair slicked down with mustard oil. Polashi was supposed to go to Monjilpur with him. He would spend the entire day with her. You never knew ... something could happen, something that might be written in his life in letters of gold.

The pain of that disappointment flooded Beji's heart again. He turned philosophical once more, saying, 'Remember what I told you one day? I'm like an open window. Heart wide open. The breeze can do what it likes. Come in, or stay outside, as it pleases. Can't force it.'

Polashi gazed at him for some time, without a word. Then, wiping the sweat and grime from her face and neck and shoulders, she said unhappily, '*Tui manush na boka patha?* Didn't I tell you I'd go with you, you fool? Yes or no? What more can a girl say? Even the girls in the trade can't say more. And now you're spouting poetry. Window, breeze, bullshit. You think the breeze is going to dig a tunnel into your heart?'

Beji was speechless. And furious at his own stupidity. A woman never allowed her tongue to reveal what was in her heart. You had to read the signs in her eyes, in her smile. Polashi wasn't coy like other women, so she had revealed a good deal, but he had been a fool, he hadn't understood. Beji wanted to bang his head on the wall.

Jumping to her feet, Polashi went off towards the lake, cupping her hands and splashing water on her burning face and eyes. She was a little thirsty. When she lived in her village, she would drink from ponds and tanks and never fall ill. But this water wasn't fit for drinking. Everyone in the locality washed their clothes and bathed here. More important, the water supplied by the corporation passed through many areas before being discharged in the lake here, which meant it was polluted by then. Diarrhoea was guaranteed if you drank it.

Returning, she found Beji perched on his sack, pondering glumly. It wasn't as though she couldn't guess what he was brooding about. Still, she said, 'What's on your mind, Beji?'

'Thinking of going home one of these days.'

'You have a home?'

'A room if not a house. My mother lives there. Keep telling her to come. She refuses. Half the people from the village are in Calcutta. No jobs there. Everyone's here in search of food. Some of them at least own land. We own nothing. Just a hut and five or six coconut trees. Enough to keep her at home. Don't care if I eat or starve, she says, won't leave home. I belong here, I'll die here—won't go away just to survive. Calcutta may be just eight hours away, but to her, it's another country. So she's there, with some hens and ducks, and a couple of goats. I go to see her sometimes. Come with me?'

'Who else is there in your family?'

'Two sisters. I got one married off nearby. She's happy. They cook twice a day. Eat fish, eat prawns. Her husband has a job with a salary. Know Herebhanga Market? Huge place. He's a sweeper there. Gets salary, plus leftovers from shops.'

'And the other sister?'

'Married too.'

'Where's she?'

'Delhi. I hear she's happy too.'

'Hear? You've never been? Never visited her?'

'Never. Couldn't. Too far. Tickets too costly.'

'How did she get married to someone from Delhi?'

'Podar-ma from our village lives in Delhi. She arranged it. Has taken girls from many villages nearby. Not enough girls there. So they take them from here to marry.'

'You should have made some enquiries before the marriage,' Polashi said, after some thought. 'These agents tell lies and take our girls to other cities. They promise marriage and good jobs. Later, you find out they've all ended up in brothels. Remember what they told Shondhya from our rail colony? You can join the movies. The family she worked for was going to send her off to some Arab country from Bombay. She's smart, so she caught on and told the police just before they were going to put her on the plane.'

'I fear something bad too,' said Beji worriedly. 'But what to do? Delhi is huge. As big as Calcutta. Where will I look for her? Don't have an address.'

'That Podar-ma. Catch hold of her. Ask her where your sister is, tell her to take you there.'

'Been two or three years now. She hasn't been coming to the village anymore. That time when she took my sister, she took some other girls too. Somewhere in Meerut. Like you said, she kept them locked up. Made them do things. Beat them up if they refused. There was one girl. Could climb trees. They were repairing the house. She climbed the scaffolding. Ran away. Came back and told everyone. Podar-ma hasn't returned since. The police went looking. Didn't find her. I'm worried about my sister. Don't know what happened to her.'

Beji couldn't go on, and Polashi didn't know what she could say. A painful wall of silence closed in around them.

Polashi was a survivor. Temptations had come her way many times. But although she had managed to save herself, she had seen many others lured to their ruin. And Beji? He knew it all too, more or less.

A long time passed this way. It wasn't personal for Polashi, so she was the first to recover. Trying to get the mood back to normal, she asked, 'So there's no one to look after burima back in the village?'

'No one.'

Crinkling her eyes and smiling slyly, Polashi said, 'No one to look after her there, no one to look after you here. You eat at hotels, sleep on the pavement. It's different for burima, she's counting her days. Not like that for you. Get married now. You're old enough. Your earnings aren't bad either. Two-fifty, three hundred a day. I'm a woman, even I make that much. You must be making more. You don't drink or do drugs—you're what they call a good boy. Plenty of girls around for you. Want to marry?'

Beji didn't reply. Things were going the right way. A little more help, Lord.

Looking meaningfully into Beji's eyes, Polashi said, 'Don't you want to marry? Don't you want someone to cook for you, serve you your dinner at the end of day, dress up for you in the evening? Aren't you drawn to a woman's body?'

Beji looked away, turning his gaze to the lake. Small waves were playing on it. He nodded. 'I am. Of course I am. But ...'

'But what?'

'Who's going to marry me? Dark, bad teeth ...'

'Have you ever asked anyone?'

Beji's voice dripped despair. 'So many. Anjoli, Komli, all of them. Can't tell you what Debi said.'

'What did she say?'

'Said, what you earn from ragpicking won't cover even my daily expense. How will you maintain me? I'll go out once a month and earn more in that day than you do all month. You'll keep me? I can keep four of you.' Beji sounded dispirited. 'Women don't care for the heart. Only the pocket.'

'Not always, Beji.' Polashi put her hand on poor Beji's back. A tender touch. 'Not all women. When they find a man they love, they can follow him anywhere. They can starve and still be in love. So many people, so few hearts.'

Enough time spent here, Polashi told herself, I should get going. Got to get this scrap weighed, then go back home and have a long bath to cool down. There was rice left over from the morning; she would eat it with some raw onions and chillies, and go to sleep. Both body and mind would recover.

She had barely hoisted her sack on her shoulder when Beji blurted out suddenly, 'Will you marry me?'

'What! What did you say?' Polashi was bemused.

In an unwavering voice, Beji repeated what he had often tried to say but failed. 'I'm asking if you'll marry me. Do you like me? Straight question. Give me a straight answer.'

Polashi felt as though Beji had thrown a rock at her head, and she was bleeding profusely. No visible wound, but she was being swept away, deep within herself. Blood was salty. Tears too. The salty flow seemed to assail her very soul and carry it away in a torrent. With great effort she resisted it.

Polashi sat for a long time like a stone. Finally, she said, 'I may not accept it, but the truth is, I must be three or four years older than you. You weren't wrong to call me didi. You're wise, you know how to show respect. It wasn't your fault. The sun cooked my brain and I spoke like a mad woman. But how can I marry someone who's like my brother?'

When she had finished, Beji said, 'I heard you out. My turn now. Listen carefully. Don't interrupt.'

'Tell me.'

'You weren't waiting with a notebook and pencil when I was born to note the time. So you can't tell for sure how old I am. I don't know myself. How do you know you're older? Maybe, maybe not. And even if you are, you must be two years older or five. The rule is, the boy must be older. Why can't it change? Who made the rule? We did. We can break it if we have to. God didn't make it. So many old things are useless now. Old weight, old coins.'

Beji had to pause to spit. Then he continued. 'We're not related by blood. What if I called you didi? Doesn't make you my sister. The word means nothing. And then take that Jolil Molla's case. Who's he married? His aunt's daughter. I've heard uncles marry nieces somewhere. And in some other place, only the eldest brother can marry; the others can't. They all make do with one woman. My point is, if it's bad, it's bad for everyone. And if it's good, it's good for everyone. If I get fever, the doctor will give me the same medicine as Jolil. If he can marry his cousin, why can't I marry you?'

Listen to his arguments. A torrent of logic. Polashi said in surprise, 'What's your point? You want me to say yes?'

'Yes. I like you a lot. Believe me. If you say yes, I won't look anywhere else. I've been wanting to tell you. For a long time. Couldn't. No chance. Now I've said it. You can be angry if you want.'

Beji was in the grip of eloquence today. The words kept gushing out. 'You know. You've said it yourself. I don't drink. Don't gamble. Don't go to whores.'

'I never said anything about whoring.'

'I don't. Swear by my mother.'

'All right.'

'Only bad habits are khoini and a little ganja. I can stop that, too, if you ask me. Now tell me. Will you marry me?'

Go on, Polashi. Say yes. He's a good boy, this Beji. Most important, he loves you so much. And you know it. You tested him the other day; he passed. He waited nearly two hours for you at the station. His anxiety, his tearful face, the way he constantly went up to the railway lines to check the road you'd take—all of this had moved Kamini. Don't make him suffer more, she had told you. Go to him if you intend to commit. Otherwise, don't raise his hopes. She had realised that day that he wasn't like the others. You're pretty, you can get anyone you want, anybody at all. But you won't get such pure love. Come on, Polashi, don't you love him? Why did you want to go out with him on the pretext of visiting the shrine? You only changed your mind to test him. Go on, say yes now—what's stopping you? Don't forget you're a woman. And not getting any younger. Turn down a meal today and you might have to starve tomorrow.

'Give me a few days to think it over,' Polashi told Beji. 'This is a big decision. Can't say yes on the spot.'

As clouds gathered on Beji's face, Polashi continued. 'Don't be upset if I don't marry you. You'll find a girl a hundred times better than me. I will find one for you.'

'Never mind others. What are you thinking?' Beji sounded impatient and annoyed.

'I can't offer you any hope right now.'

He had heard what had to be heard, understood what had to be understood. Sadly, Beji hoisted his sack on his shoulder, his voice revealing acerbity and regret. 'Are you going? I am,' he said, and marched off. Polashi had expected him to look back at least once, but he didn't.

The flaming sun overhead, the heated earth underfoot, and the fire in his heart, all raised Beji's emotional temperature well above normal. The weight of his heavy sack no longer impeded him. He walked swiftly, arriving after some time at a fork in the road, where one arm meandered southwards, and the other led to Rambabur Baajar, Kayostho Polli and Babu Bagan.

Beji saw Gopal running furiously towards him up the second road, as though chased by a wild bull. He kept looking over his shoulder as he ran. His sack was no longer on his shoulder. But he did have his rod, which was pointed at one end and hooked at the other.

Of all those who sold scrap to Paanu, Gopal was the only one to be seen with a rod. No one was as fearless, no one could wield a rod with such skill. Gopal himself acknowledged it needed guts, but how else could you expect to earn cold cash?

What Gopal carried was not so much a rod as something like a solid cylindrical pipe, though much thinner. But he was known as a 'rodbaaj' because of his excessive fondness for women. Just the other day, he had told Beji, 'Fate has made you a bachelor, and me a "fuckelor". Done over a hundred already.'

The rod was two-and-a-half-feet long, with a hook at one end. The other end tapered to a point, which he used to pin scraps of paper or plastic on the ground and put them in his sack. With the hook he reached through open windows and gathered whatever he could. There was no counting the number of saris and petticoats and blouses and trousers and shirts he had hooked this way. If luck smiled on him, he even got a watch or a gold necklace sometimes. The women of the slum hung around him to buy saris cheap.

Not that Gopal took money from all of them. If he liked someone, and she liked him back, he gave her saris and petticoats free. But to prove that she really liked him, a woman had to follow him into the darkness in the undergrowth next to the sewage pipes behind the hospital. On the days Gopal snagged a sari, he bathed with soap, backbrushed his hair, and took up position behind the railway station. Whenever he spotted a woman he fancied, he would go up to her and whisper, 'Got a gorgeous sari today. Thinking of giving it to you.'

If she said, 'To me? Give it then. When will you give it? Can't wait', Gopal would answer, 'I was thinking right now, but it's not with me, it's at my brother-in-law's place. He rents a room near Hori Singh's cowshed, you know, next to the ink company? If you want it right now, you have to come with me.'

Gopal always got good, expensive saris, which people here could not afford. The woman would get apprehensive. Gopal knows many girls. If I say no, what if he gives it to someone else? It's happened in the past.

So she might say, 'All right, I have nothing important to do right now. I'll get to meet your sister too.'

Gopal would then lead her beyond the broken-down wall around the hospital compound and walk eastwards. Behind the hospital was the sewage canal, on the other side of which lived the babus. They would walk to the south, along the canal, into the undergrowth, where Gopal would tell her, 'Not asking you to pay for the sari, but you have to give me something in return for it.' He would even add dialogue from Hindi films. *'Kuchh paane ke liye kuchh khona parta hai.'* Most of the women, especially those who were experienced in such matters, gave in. If they didn't, Gopal sent them back to the station empty-handed. 'Go away—there are enough women who want a sari. I thought you might like it. But since you don't, you can go.'

Still, Gopal never tried to do anything by force to a woman alone in the dark. Which was why he had not yet been beaten up. Though he did get into trouble once, and escaped a thrashing by the skin of his teeth.

Joya, who had been abandoned by her husband, lived in no. 1 rail bosti. Gopal had set a bait for her, and she had created trouble instead of swallowing it. But things didn't get far because of a lack of public support. Feeling deprived and let down, she had turned for justice to the twin sisters Shoptomi and Ashtomi from the rail bosti, famous for starting arguments and fights. 'You know what that fucking rodbaaj told me?' Joya had complained. 'Said, come behind the trees, I'll give you a sari. How dare he? I'm married, I'm a respectable woman. My bhaatar may not take me into his home today, but tomorrow he will. He didn't even think twice. I want justice.' After listening to all the details, Ashtomi had said, 'He doesn't have what you have. You don't have what he has. So he wanted an exchange. It didn't work; the price wasn't right. He didn't give you anything; you didn't give him anything. End of story. He's committed no crime, nor have you. Nothing to judge. It would have been different if he'd forced you. We would have had Gopal thrashed outside the station. Nothing to be done here.'

Joya had tried complaining to a couple of others, too, but got no support, so things hadn't got out of hand. In fact, it had worked to Gopal's advantage. Now everyone knew he had saris to give away; you just had to be willing to pay the right price.

Beji stopped on seeing Gopal running towards him, gasping for breath. He realised that Gopal was frightened. But before he could say anything, it was Gopal who asked, 'Why so late today?'

Beji said, 'I was resting by the lake—it's so hot. Where's your sack?'

Gopal smiled in embarrassment. 'Dropped it and ran away. Wouldn't have escaped if I brought it with me.'

'Dropped it! Why?'

'You think I could have run as fast if I was carrying it? No chance. Those bastards would have caught me for sure.'

He explained without being asked, 'There was a watch on the desk in a house I was passing by. The owner had put it there and gone for a bath. I stuck my rod in. It would have been in my hand in a moment, but I ran out of luck. Someone entered the room and saw me, and began to shout. I had to drop my sack and run. Fuckers chased me all the way, wouldn't let go. Made me run a mile. Lucky I didn't get caught, or I'd have been in hospital by now.'

'Better not go on your rounds for a couple of months,' Beji advised.

Polashi was lagging behind. She hadn't been walking as quickly as Beji because she wasn't driven by rage or despair. But since he had stopped to talk to Gopal, she caught up with him. A dishevelled Gopal was there, too, but it wasn't because he wanted to talk to her. He was terrified; what if they were on his tail with a motorbike? So he practically ran towards the station. 'I'll see you later.' Going up to Beji, Polashi asked, 'What's happened to Gopal, why's he running like that?'

'How should I know? Ask him yourself.' Beji had no wish to converse with the heartless Polashi. He threw the words at her as he walked off.

'He told you.'

'So?'

'You won't tell me?'

'No.'

'Are you angry with me?'

'No. What for? Who cares if I am?'

Polashi didn't bother who might be looking. Grabbing Beji's hair and pulling his head down, she gave him a smacking kiss on his sweaty face. 'Don't be angry, my darling, I love you so much. I'll be very upset if you're angry. You don't know everything about me, never had the chance to tell you. We meet for a few minutes on the road; there's no time to talk. If I can go somewhere with you for a couple of days, if you take me, I can tell you everything properly.'

Beji was speechless. The spot where she had kissed him was tingling. A sudden gift, the first touch of a woman's lips. He was over the moon. Lugging his sack, he continued to walk.

Walking alongside, Polashi said, 'Is marriage all there is to life? I've never hankered for it, or I could have married long ago—I'm not ugly. Men stare at me all the time, I can tell. One of them grabbed my feet and wept, wouldn't go away from my door. I felt pity, but I couldn't say yes.'

After a pause, she exhaled loudly and continued: 'If I marry you, if you marry me, we'll be tethered to each other, like a cow to a post. Yes or no? I don't like being tied to anyone. Don't go here, don't look there, don't do this, don't do that—I can't stand so many rules. So many girls from the bosti work in the babus' houses. They live in comfort, don't have to go out come rain or shine, and it shows on their bodies. I don't do it because it means following orders. I live off my own earnings, I don't wait on anyone—I'm my own boss. I like living this way.'

A little later, Polashi nudged Beji. 'Well? Say something. I'm the one doing all the talking.'

'You're talking. I'm listening. Two can't talk at the same time.'

'I know at least twenty girls who had lavish weddings. Not one of them is happy. All back to their parents within two or three years, one child in their arms, one at the hip, one in the belly. Some get beaten up by their father-in-law and mother-in-law, some are forced to sleep with their brothers-in-law, and some are sent by their husbands to sleep with other men. What I've seen has made me sick of marriage. Imagine tolerating such torture just for that little bit of sidoor in your hair. I'm my own boss, no one has the right to order me around.

'Fuck it. I have to work like a dog now, I'll have to work like a dog then, too. No one's going to bathe my feet like a rich man's wife. It's different for them, they don't have to lift a finger. One order and six people come running to serve tea or a cold drink, to do their hair, to help them dress. Those who marry them have only one requirement. You can hire someone for everything except that one thing. Where will they go if they want to fuck at midnight. So they've got someone near at hand. It's not like that for us. Start slaving at dawn, clean-cook-serve, and then go make some money too. And yet my body isn't mine. I cannot feel any pain. My yes and no are worthless. On my back, on my belly, on my knees, I'll be fucked as he pleases. Why? That sidoor. Gives him every right. Stick your dick up your sidoor. Don't want it in my hair. What fucking difference will it make to my life?'

Polashi's tongue was a lethal weapon. Beji was incensed. Hotly, he said, 'What're you telling me all this for? Do you think I'm one of them?'

Polashi realised she had overdone it. It was true—why did she have to say all this to him? They were from different camps, with contrasting views. Beji had seen no less of the world than she had. He knew as much as she did. Just that their views were from opposite sides of the river.

She couldn't keep pace with Beji and had fallen far behind. Beji's anger was driving him. Polashi only felt sympathy for him. Now she heard a rickshaw honking over her shoulder. It was Ganjati Gonesh. There was another Gonesh in the area, a drunkard. He was called Cholai Gonesh. Both of them were bastards who inevitably said dirty things to her. Now, Ganjati Gonesh grinned lasciviously at her and said, 'Gimme, Polashi, gimme a little.'

Polashi felt a fuse go off in her head. 'Fuck your father, you son of a bitch! What will I give you?'

'Why so angry? I wasn't suggesting anything bad. I was only asking for your sack. I'm headed that way, I could take it.'

'You think I don't know what you're suggesting? See my slippers? I'll take your skin off.'

Since his efforts weren't working, the rickshaw-driver pedalled ahead quickly, chanting in a sing-song tone, 'Kisses for the rest, nothing for the best.' Polashi's choicest expletives chased him on his way.

There wasn't a long way left to go; One-Armed Paanu's scrapyard came into view. Paanu wasn't there, but one of his employees was: the one who had replaced Moharaj. The ragpickers were converging from different directions. An enormous pair of scales stood in front of the yard, where all the scavenged material was being weighed before it was taken inside. Scraps of paper, plastic, pieceboard, iron pieces—all that was once purchased with money but then discarded—were gathered and deposited by those who lived off scavenging.

One-Armed Paanu was a decent man, no matter how much he was prone to letting his tongue fly. He was kind. He had raised the price he paid by fifty paise per kilo without being asked. That meant an additional twenty rupees for forty kilos, which no other scrap-dealer offered. Which was why everyone sold to Paanu. 'If I make two rupees thanks to all of you, why shouldn't I give you one rupee out of it.' The others had got their share, of course, but it was Beji's day—he'd made a killing.

Beji was known by his real name Brojonath, or Brojo, for several years after his arrival in Calcutta. It had changed to Beji somehow after that. He came from a village near Basanti, where he might well have remained if his father hadn't been devoured by a crocodile. All there was back home, by way of assets, was the shack where his mother lived. They had never owned any land, only a couple of ducks and hens and a few goats. There was a cow once, but it was gone. His father used to work very hard. A fearless man, he would go fishing by himself. On that occasion, he was trying to catch fish with a small net, and, in fact, had some companions with him. What he didn't know was that a hungry crocodile was lying in wait. It had seized Beji's father's leg in its jaws and dragged him into the water before anyone could react. Hard days had descended on Beji and his mother after this. She would gather wild roots and vegetables and snails and shellfish. Mother and son would assuage their hunger by boiling these and eating them with salt.

Beji was fifteen or sixteen at the time. That was when someone told him, 'Neither you nor your mother will survive if you stay here. Take my advice, your mother and you should go to Calcutta. You'll find money flying on the streets there.'

Beji was young but not naive. He knew it wasn't literally money that was to be found on the streets, but something that could fetch money. He had decided right then to move but hadn't got round to it. Calcutta was a distant land, after all, where he knew no one.

Beji finally made it to Calcutta in the year of the devastating storm Ayla. Everyone whose home had been swept away was making a beeline for the state capital. With prospects of farming gone, they were hoping for some work—any work—that would help them survive. Beji and another young man left for Calcutta eventually. His companion reassured him, 'No need to worry about where to live. You can live in the station. Hundreds of people live there.'

They took a train from Canning and got off at this station, staying here for two days and two nights, roaming around everywhere in search of work, but without success. There were some rules when it came to looking for work, but they had no idea of this.

Still, whether there was work to be found during the day or not, there was always a chance of making a little money early in the morning, when the fish train from Canning stopped at Jadavpur. Two hundred or more fish traders got off the train here every morning with their fish baskets before dispersing to various markets.

That day, Beji was carrying a basket of fish to the market in Bagharmor. On his way back, after collecting his payment, he was stopped by someone outside the dilapidated mosque in Kanjipara. The man was soaked in sweat, and smelling of it. The shirt and lungi he was dressed in were not torn, but filthy. Grime was sticking to every pore in his body. And yet he was chewing on a fragrant paan, with jorda.

Spitting out the juice, he said to Beji, 'Carry a sack for me? You know Paanu's scrapyard by the railway siding? You have to take it there. I'll pay two rupees.'

Beji examined the sack, which looked enormous. 'You think I can do it by myself?' he asked apprehensively.

'Of course. If I can, why can't you? Only asking you because I hurt my leg. Or I'd have taken it yesterday. A sack this size won't fit on the rickshaw.'

'What's in the sack?' asked Beji.

The man laughed, showing red stains on his teeth. 'What's in the sack? Money, that's what, money.' Beji was astonished. A sack of this size filled with money? How much money was that? And imagine just leaving it by the road all night—what if someone took it?

The stranger continued without being asked, 'People throw it away; I pick it up and put it in my sack. Haven't you heard the streets of Calcutta are full of money? That's what this is.'

Beji had hoisted the sack of 'money' on his shoulder with great curiosity. Two rupees was far too little considering the distance, but he was driven by his interest in the whole thing. And then he had seen for himself this money that was gathered from the streets.

It took nearly half an hour to reach Paanu's scrapyard. Beji lowered the sack to the ground, and its owner opened the mouth to pour everything out. It was stuffed with torn slippers, broken plastic buckets, empty liquor bottles, rusted iron rods, and, most of all, paper scraps. An astonishing sight. The man sorted the iron, plastic, glass and paper into separate piles, and then put each of them on the scales to be weighed. The price varied according to the material. When he was done measuring, he counted out his takings. Eight and four, twelve ... add six ... that's eighteen. Eighteen plus seven is ... nineteen twenty twenty-one twenty-two twenty-three twenty-four twenty-five. So a total of twenty-five, that was his earning from a full day's labour yesterday. So much money! Beji's father would work like a bull and never make more than five rupees a day. And this man had only done the rounds of the streets with his sack and made twenty-five!

Beji had told the man all about why he was in Calcutta. He had replied, 'Why don't you ask Paanu-da for a sack. Go out on your rounds. One round from morning to afternoon, one later. But don't enter my territory. Like they say, if someone's starving, give them something to eat, don't teach them how to earn. I've shown you the way, but if you try to stab me in the back, I won't spare you. From the 8B bus-stand to Bagharmor via the Srinath Colony market on the Santoshpur road, that's my beat. You can cover up to Mukundapur from Palpara, via Santoshpur. Nobody permanent there. Some people from the Bondel Gate side drift in here sometimes, but they're up to no good with their logibaaji. I'm going to bash them up one of these days.'

The 'logibaajs' were like rodbaajs, Beji had learnt later. All the ragpickers were involved in it to some extent. There were even some who trafficked in illegal goods.

And so, Beji took the well-meant advice and joined the line, touring the streets with his sack and collecting discarded scrap. Starting with ten rupees a day, he now made up to three hundred. He was happy with his work. He was nobody's servant; he was free, and self-reliant. It was just that he felt lonely. His heart cried for a companion. He had made a throne, but there was no one to install on it. No one would have been happier than Beji if Polashi had accepted his proposal.

Now, he slammed his sack to the ground in rage at being rejected. A metallic sound rang out, informing everyone nearby that Beji had hit the jackpot today. Emptying his sack, he selected the iron rods and put them on the scales. He had hoped for twenty-five kilos, but it turned out to be just eighteen. He put the rest of his scrap on the scale and collected his money. Without a look or a word for Polashi, who was standing nearby, he tucked the money into the waist of his lungi and walked off, his slippers flapping loudly.

One of Polashi's closest friends was Kamini. She was a ragpicker, too, who disappeared at intervals after getting married, only to return in some time after calling it off. She had been all over India in this way. The last time she came back, it was from Punjab, where she had been with a truck driver. On her return, she had told Polashi, 'We have fish-and-rice bodies. Couldn't deal with a Punjabi bhaatar, so I ran away.'

A few days after her return from Punjab, Kamini revealed the high points of her experience. 'Odias or Marwaris or

Punjabis, whatever you may say, there can be no better bhaatars than Bengalis. Even the worst Bengali bhaatar is better than the best from any other region. Bengalis have kind hearts. They consider their wives their family; they don't make impossible demands on them. When the others grab you, it's like a tiger mauling a lamb—they won't let you go till they've chewed you up. I've tried them all out. I'm not going away again. If I find a Bengali after my own heart, I'll marry one last time. Then I don't care if he wants to kill me or eat me up—I'll stick with him all my life. And if I don't find someone like that, I won't marry at all.'

'You did marry a Bengali once, why did you leave him?' asked Polashi.

'I was young then, didn't know what was what. That shitface used to love me a lot, but he had no earnings. Gambled all day. You can't live on love, can you? Besides, I didn't know how to make any money, so I left him. It wasn't me that ran away, it was my hunger. Then for ten years I took up with another man, then left him. Took up with another, then left him. Every time, I felt it would be better than the last time. And every time I found out, no, it was worse, I might get food and clothes, but the way I was tormented was worse than death.'

Polashi and Kamini had these heart-to-heart talks all the time. So Kamini knew everything in Polashi's heart; she understood her nature and her thinking. When she saw Beji walk off in a huff, she asked Polashi, 'What's the matter, have you quarrelled with him? Why's Beji looking so glum? It's not like him.'

Polashi smiled ruefully. 'The donkey wants to die young. Says he wants to marry me. I didn't agree, so babu is disappointed. He's asking for death without realising it; should I kill him? Will God forgive me? You think the idiot can actually live with me? He'll be hurt every step of the way.'

Kamini grimaced. 'Why should Beji die if he marries you? You got syphilis?'

'Bitch!' Polashi snarled. 'Why should I have syphilis? *You* have syphilis. Didn't you marry a driver? They go everywhere—eat at every table. He gave it to you.'

Kamini didn't lose her temper at this because Polashi was smiling.

After a pause, Polashi said, 'Women and men—so different. A woman can take it if her bhaatar has other women, but a man can't if his wife so much as smiles at another man. I can't change the way I live, can I? It'll just mean quarrels and shouting and fights. And then it'll be over. Better not to marry. Beji loves me, let him—I'm not stopping him. All I'm saying is, I'm a free bird, I'm not getting into a cage. I said, fly with me instead. The donkey won't agree.'

Sky, bird, cage—Kamini found it familiar. She'd heard it all somewhere. Was it on the radio?

She couldn't remember for sure, but there was another dialogue she did recollect, which she promptly recycled. 'Look, Polashi, we girls, we can fly high, but we're actually vines; we need to wrap ourselves around something: a big tree. How long can we be birds flying from one branch to another? Only as long as we're young. What I say is, if

Beji wants to marry you, say yes. Settle down. Enough of flying around.'

'Oh, you want me to settle down while *you* keep flying?'

The conversation couldn't go any further, because one of the twins had joined them. Short, dark and bony, Ashtomi said, 'Come quick! Big fight at the station.' She enjoyed watching fights as much as she enjoyed fighting herself. Sometimes she even threw herself into the fray to defend the weaker side.

But neither Kamini nor Polashi was enthused by the news. Nothing new—the vicinity of the station was prone to violence. What did anyone expect from the place, peace marches? Fights broke out here over a hand in someone's pocket, an elbow in someone's face, a nudge on someone's shoulder. Noses were broken, scalps were split, chins were bruised. Where unhappy, dissatisfied people gather, skirmishes are a daily offer.

Ashtomi was miffed at neither of them giving her news any importance. Furiously, she said, 'Someone's going to be killed. We'll all be fucked. Dopdi's husbands are at each other's throats. They won't stop till one of them is dead. Who knows whose arse the police will take when they get here.'

Everyone around was forced to pay attention now. There were many people from the slums here. If someone was killed, the police would definitely go on the rampage. The residents of the two rail bostis were never treated humanely. The police had nothing but loathing and contempt for them, and were always looking for ways to pin one person's crime on another. If one of Dopdi's husbands murdered the other and vanished—which was almost a hundred per cent likely—there was no reason for someone else not to be framed.

Dopdi had earned this particular name from the residents of the slum because the count of her husbands had once come close to matching her mythical namesake Droupadi's. Dopdi, who was from no. 1 bosti, hadn't wanted to live in the same house as her husband's second wife. Angry with her husband for his new marriage, she had left their village home in Gosaba for Calcutta, telling him, 'If you can, so can I! Which holy books say men can and women can't? If they do, I piss on them.' After moving to Calcutta, she had married two men within the year, after which she sent word to her husband in Gosaba—'Come to Calcutta, you'll see I can do everything that you can.'

The two husbands with whom she lived nowadays were from Bihar and Odisha, respectively. Her very first husband was a Bengali, with whom her wedding had been solemnised by a priest. The man she then ran away with and married was a Bengali too. Her two current husbands had wives and children of their own back home. They had done the calculations—it was cheaper to share a wife than to hire maids.

Both of them worked as watchmen at the same factory. Between them, they had worked out a schedule so that one of them would be on night duty while the other one spent the night at home. Several years had passed peacefully this way, so what had happened suddenly today for them to get into a fight, which threatened to end in murder?

Ashtomi explained everything. One of them had said: I was the first among us to have taken up with Dopdi, so the child in her womb is mine, I will be considered its father. The other one had countered: you may have been the first, but Dopdi got pregnant while you were away in your village. So the child is mine, I'm the father. This was what had led to the fisticuffs.

'What's Dopdi saying? She should know who the father is.'

'Dopdi says it'll hurt whichever arm is cut off. Both are the father, one senior and one junior.'

'That solves the problem.'

'It does not. The problem remains unchanged. Now both of them want to be the senior father. How can anyone solve this?'

Some more time passed in giggling over this. The scrap had been weighed and the payment made, it was time to go. But not to watch the fight. The heat was killing them; it was time for a bath. Kamini and Polashi lived near each other. They left together.

To the left of an open field where a temporary market came up every evening, appropriately called shondhebaajar, was a pond with fetid water. Posts driven into its bottom supported a platform, on which stood about thirty shacks. Jadavpur Railway Station was on its right. Kamini and Polashi were approaching the shacks.

'All the shops are closed,' said Kamini. 'Need to buy soap. How to bathe without soap?'

'Bitch!' hissed Polashi. 'Whore of a hundred bhaatars! You think I don't get your tricks? Just say it straight: Polashi, let me use your soap.'

Kamini smiled as though she'd been caught stealing. 'Don't be late, okay? Get your clothes and come to the pond quickly.'

Polashi had only one task now—bathe as quickly as possible. She didn't plan to cook. The rice she had soaked in water in the morning would have turned sour by now. It would taste delicious with green chillies and onions on a summer day like this.

As they were walking past the shacks, a middle-aged man dashed out from wherever he had been lurking and blocked Polashi's way. Bewildered by this sudden appearance, she blurted out, 'Sonofabitch!' Polashi was seeing him after a long time. He hadn't been around for the past six months.

Grabbing Polashi's arm, he growled like a gratified pig. 'Found you after a long time. Not letting you go today, rani.'

'Let go of my hand, you whelp of a whore, it hurts. Just got new bangles yesterday, you better not smash them, all right?' Speaking with a mixture of feigned anger and real affection, Polashi continued: 'And where were you getting your arse fucked all these days? I thought you were dead. But even death doesn't give a fuck about you.'

'I was in Bangladesh,' he said. 'I'd never been back since I escaped during the '71 war. I had a little land left there, so I went to sell it off. An agent took me across. But I got caught by the BSF on my way back, so that needed twenty thousand. Not going back anymore. No need to. Spent eight thousand here on a voter card and ration card. Now I'm going to buy a bit of land, maybe in Gopalnagar or Hosseinpur, build a house, and live there forever.'

'No plans to marry? Or do you plan to remain a bachelor and paw other men's wives?'

'Of course I'll marry. Let the business stand on its feet first. A trader in Kolay Market has told me to take as much material as I want and pay him after it's sold.'

Polashi sniggered. 'You're over forty already. By the time the business stands on its feet, the other thing won't stand anymore. What use getting married then?'

'Six months, that's all,' said the man, 'the business will be up and running by then. Find a pretty girl for me, I'll give you a sari as your fee.'

'What sort of a girl?'

'Someone pretty. Like you. I really like you, but you don't want to marry. But fuck that, come with me now.'

'Where?'

'To my shack. Where else?'

Polashi tried to free her arm. 'Are you mad? In this heat, in the middle of the afternoon? I'm sweating all over, my clothes are stinking. I have to bathe.'

'If you're sweating, have I got perfume on? Am I smelling of flowers? Come for a bit, I beg of you. It's been so long—don't turn me down. I promise not to take too long—you'll be back in no time.

The man began to drag Polashi towards the shacks. Unable to shake him off, she looked helplessly at Kamini.

Desperately, she said, 'It's like a first meal for a starving man. This maachod won't let me go. Carry on. I'll meet you with the soap. You understand, don't you? Don't be angry.'

Polashi was led to one of the shacks by the strength and 'love' of the man she had just called a motherfucker. Sacks of potatoes were piled inside, with just a sliver of space remaining in the shack next to them. There was a table-fan too, running on illegally tapped electricity. The man spent nights in this room, guarding the potatoes, but he had made living arrangements too. The door closed as soon as they went in.

5

At the heart of any successful operation lies close observation. Along with practice and patience—waiting for the right time. The man who had articulated this piece of wisdom was widely respected. Mohaguru Roton Mukherjee. Every tingbaaj in business considered this utterance gospel truth. For he never spoke in vain. Nothing he said was just for effect—it was the essence of twenty years of experience. Surviving two decades in the tingbaaji business was no small achievement. Most of those who had tried their hand at it had given up after a couple of years. But Guru Roton Mukherjee was, is, and will be in this business forever.

The most important thing was that he had not hoarded the expertise he had acquired—he had patiently built a band of followers and disciples who were thriving on the skills they had learnt from their mentor.

Guru Roton Mukherjee's territory stretched from Diamond Harbour, Lakshmikantapur and Canning all the way to Sealdah. He reigned over all the iron wheels that rolled on this particular line. The son of a bitch who could challenge his monopoly had not yet been born.

Everyone said Roton Mukherjee's right hand should be preserved for eternity. It wasn't so much a hand as a magic wand—anything it touched turned to gold. With long years of training, Roton babu had built a small, disciplined and worthy cadre, who addressed him as 'ostad' in his presence, and as 'headmistri' behind his back.

Many people say theft is an elevated art. When he heard this, Roton babu sneered, 'That's no art. The mother of all arts is the one we practise. It's easy to steal things from a room with a corpse, but that's chicanery. The real art is ours, which we perform in full view of people. We fool people like a magician does.'

He could still be tolerant of petty criminals like the gaabbaaj, the dholbaaj or the porhibaaj, but Roton babu couldn't stand robbers. 'Do you call them human? The bastards are worse than beasts. It's one thing to grab a man's hard-earned money, but to shoot him dead when he tries to stop you—is human life so cheap to you? What's the difference between you and salaried policemen then? You're protecting your own interests—have you spared a thought for the man's wife and children? How will they survive?'

That year when there were floods in Medinipur, when Munna Mahato's parents were swept away, his uncle grabbed whatever he could of the family's possessions, escorted Munna to the station, put him on the train without a ticket, and said, 'Go wherever the hell you want. Come back here and I'll bury you alive. With salt!'

Munna knew his uncle was perfectly capable of this. Those days, there was an active programme of burying people alive. This was the main plank of partybaaji—if you don't follow my orders, if you oppose me, I'll bury you alive. Rumour had it that Munna's uncle was called away in the middle of the night on a similar mission. He had a bullock-cart. Munna had spotted blood on it in the morning. Crows were pecking away at the dark blood clots.

'What are you staring at?' Munna's uncle had snarled at him. He had run away without risking a backward glance.

There was another orphan like Munna, whose name was Protap. Whenever he felt hungry, he set out under cover of darkness to steal. A ripe papaya from someone's tree, bananas from someone else's, cucumbers, coconuts, sugarcane, watermelon—he would steal anything he could lay his hands on. A couple of times he had been caught and beaten up badly, but still he hadn't stopped.

One morning he told Munna about his chilling experience of going out to steal the night before. 'Promise not to tell anyone, Munna. I won't tell you otherwise.'

'Tell me what?'

'What I saw for myself yesterday.'

'What did you see?'

'First, give me your word you won't tell anyone.'

'I won't.'

'Swear?'

'Swear.'

'Don't be frightened, though it's very frightening.'

'Ghosts? Did you see a ghost?'

'Not a ghost at all, a human. I saw your uncle last night. It was pitch dark, but I could recognise him.'

Protap was looking absolutely terrified. He was unaware of the outcome of witnessing what he had, and unable to digest the experience. So he simply had to tell someone. What he told Munna was that he had spotted a luscious bunch of bananas in Ghosh babu's garden a few days earlier. They were wrapped in gunny cloth to prevent birds from pecking at them. He had decided to steal them once they ripened fully.

Yesterday, he was overcome by the thought of consuming those bananas. Not that anyone would acknowledge it as hunger; they would only call it a tendency to steal. Protap hadn't eaten anything much all day, not since the single mouthful of dalia he'd been given for transporting several buckets of water for the Anganwadi cook. It was like sprinkling a couple of drops of water on a raging fire. By evening his stomach was revolting in hunger.

Protap was about as old as Munna, fourteen or fifteen. But he spoke like a professional storyteller, stretching out the introduction to a point where an impatient Munna said, 'No need for all these details, what did you see?'

'That's what I'm telling you. Now, how am I to get to Ghosh babu's garden? The main road is the direct route, but in the evening, it's filled with party people carrying guns. They're afraid of retaliation from those whose villages they've terrorised. I've seen them dressed for battle, going off somewhere, bringing back people they have captured and beating them up. Wouldn't you be afraid if you saw all this, Munna? ... So yesterday what I did was, I left the village, went down to the fields in the north and into Roy babu's mustard field—I was planning to go up to the bridge at Jelekhali. The canal has very little water at this time. I would cross on foot, creep into Ghosh babu's garden, cut the bananas, and return the same way.'

'What about kaka?'

'So when I got to the bridge, I found your Anup kaka by the canal, with three or four others. It was full moon, as bright as daylight. I recognised your uncle easily, though not the others. They were probably from some other village.'

'What was kaka doing there?'

'Digging a hole.'

'A hole!'

'Yes, an enormous one. I hid beneath the bridge as soon as I saw him. I was afraid he'd see me and beat me up ... So what did I see a little later?'

'What did you see?'

'They dug the hole and filled it with salt. They had brought two sacks of salt in a bullock-cart. Then you know what I saw? Two men being unloaded from the cart, all tied up. One of them was asking for water. They pushed them into the hole and then dumped a sack of salt over them. Then they filled the hole, pulled up clumps of grass from everywhere, and put them on the earth they had dug up. Poured some water to make it look neat—no one could tell a hole had been dug.' Lowering his voice, Protap continued, 'You know these two parties are fighting in Keshpur and Garbeta. Dozens of people are killed or injured every day. Some of them are buried here.'

'How do you know they're from Keshpur?'

'I'm guessing. That's what your Anup kaka and the others were saying.'

After this, Munna began to fear his uncle more than he would a wild animal. So when his Anup kaka led him to the station, he didn't dare protest.

The train for Calcutta stopped at Sealdah Station. Unable to decide where to get off or why, Munna Mahato had been sitting in a corner, overwhelmed, and fallen asleep at some point. Now, feeling like a fish tossed from a small pond into a big ocean, he didn't even dare leave the station. He had no ticket, and had just watched another passenger who couldn't produce a ticket being dragged away by several men in khaki, along with two men in black coats. Just a few days ago, Chetan Murmu had been taken away from the market back in the village in the same way by men in khaki. He had never come back; his corpse had. Munna was terrified—what if they were taking the passenger without a ticket to a hole in the ground packed with salt? He shrank back in his bench, weeping, when someone came up and sat down beside him.

A stocky man with close-cropped hair. Beady eyes and the smell of hooch on his breath. Softly he asked, 'Where did you spring from?'

Munna was familiar with the smell of alcohol; he wasn't particularly afraid of drunkards. But he was frightened by the man's appearance and the look in his eyes. Looking at the man fearfully, he said in his earthy accent, 'I don't understand what you're saying.'

'I'm asking where you've come from.'

'Medinipur.'

'East or West?'

'I don't know. Everyone calls it Medinipur.'

'Got cash?'

'What's that?'

'Don't know cash? What an idiot! Money! Got any?'

The man tried to reassure Munna. 'You can tell me the truth, I'm not such a bad man. Anyone else would have taken you to the siding, taken your clothes off, and searched you. He'd have taken every last thing and given you a kick in the backside. I won't do that. I'll take some, and leave some with you. I can do anything I like. I can sell you to the hijres at Bondel Gate. They'll pay a couple of thousand. You know what they'll do? They'll cut your cock off with a knife, then dress you in a sari and take you in. You won't be a boy anymore, you won't be a girl either. Should I ... take you there?'

Munna was utterly terrified now. The man continued, 'Or there's the beggars' camp in Park Circus. Gabbar chacha is their leader. I can sell you to them too. They'll blind you, break your arms and legs, then make you beg on the road or at the station. So which one will it be, hijra mahalla or bhikhari thek? And if you don't want either, give me everything you've got, quick.'

'I have nothing.' Munna burst into tears.

'Nothing?' The man looked astonished. 'I can tell you're a smart one. Must have stolen something and run away. They always come to Calcutta from Medinipur, and from Calcutta they run away to Bombay. You haven't stolen anything?'

'No, I haven't.'

'Then what the fuck have you come to Calcutta for?'

So Munna told him the story of his life. His parents had been swept away, his uncle had taken whatever there was and bundled him into the train. Munna didn't mention the hole in the ground and the salt.

'Can't I get work here? I can plough, I can thresh, I can break stones.'

'Not that sort of work. There's other work. But who's going to give you any work? No one knows you—what if you steal something and run away?'

'I won't do that. I'm afraid of stealing.'

The man was Roton Mukherjee. But both his surname and the poite slung around his body were fake. By virtue of being considered a Brahmin, he had often been spared a thrashing when he was caught picking someone's pocket. There were many ways to avoid being beaten up too badly. Screaming and wailing only made things worse. But, I haven't eaten for two days; I ran a shop on the pavement, the corporation demolished it; my father is ill, I don't have money for medicines—lines like these lessened the blows. And the most effective strategy was to clutch your chest and collapse on the ground, holding your breath, pretending to have fainted. Someone might still go on beating you, but you mustn't move or jump, for that would only make it worse. Roton babu was partial to this tactic, always ensuring that his poite was on view before he hit the ground.

Roton used to work on the north line at the time, doing his work on the Bongaon train. But because he'd become a known face, with the railway police having identified him and put up his photograph on the walls of the police stations, he had been forced to move to the south line. He had his cohort of thekbaajes. Their job was to crowd around the potential target so that the headmistri could do his job, and then to get rid of the stolen goods afterwards. Roton had made arrangements for his thekbaajes to live in a rented room in Kasba, a properly built structure, with a permanent roof and toilet. He paid the rent, but never stayed there himself, never let anyone know his address either. Whenever he suspected anyone from his gang of having found out where he lived, he either changed his address, or changed the gang member.

Today Roton Mukherjee was feeling generous, so he took Munna under his wing. 'Come with me, I'll get you work. The first month, you have to watch and learn. No pay now, but you'll get food and a place to stay. Once you've learnt, you'll get the same share as everyone else. It's sound work. If you learn it diligently, you can be an expert mistri in a year. And then, if you earn for yourself, you can maintain not one but two whores. That's what I tell all the thekbaajes: learn and work for yourself—do you want to remain in my gang forever?'

'What work?' Munna had asked.

Roton said, 'Seen those insects that always stick to cows? That's the work. We'll get into a crowded train, and when I give you the signal, you'll have to stick to the person I point to, and you mustn't move an inch. The rest is up to me.'

Munna Mahato no longer spoke in the Medinipur dialect. The language he used was not even Bangla. It was the coded jargon of criminals—not to be found in any dictionary, its true meaning incomprehensible even when uttered in the presence of a thousand people. So, the lock on the door was a flower. The crowbar used to break this lock, a towel. A torch referred to eyes. And people at large, their targets, were dhoors. There were two kinds of pickpockets—the one who used only their fingers was a 'tingbaaj', and the one who slit pockets with blades was a 'ghaobaaj'. Someone who broke open a flower with a towel to steal from a house was a 'gabbabaaj', while the thief who stole luggage from trains was a 'dholbaaj'.

Roton Mukherjee had given his team an English name, the 'Gang of Four'. One of them was from Piali—he was Roton's wife's brother—who used to sell Pocha Company's ginger-flavoured water on trains. Pocha was the nickname of the owner of the company—his formal name was Ponchanon. A bottle of water cost two rupees, with the profit being shared between the owner and the hawker. Roton had persuaded his brother-in-law to give up this work and join him instead. 'What sort of bullshit business is this where you can't make a hundred a day. Work with me. All you have to do is stick your cock to people's arses and stand still. I'll make sure you get your hundred whether I make any money or not.'

There was a woman in the gang too. Chandona used to work as an ayah in a nursing home somewhere. Now she had given up that job and joined Roton to earn five times as much. Back home she had two daughters and a husband who had lost both his legs. Sometimes she went home to hand over some money, claiming to be on night duty when asked about her absence by the other tenants in the building she lived in. When Roton's brother-in-law Kalipodo went home to Piali, that, too, was night duty. Their neighbours in Kasba knew Kalipodo and Chandona as husband and wife. Which was not untrue in a sense, for their relationship was just that. It had happened after moving into this house.

Chandona's husband was effectively paralysed from the waist down, and Kalipodo's wife had left him. The inevitable had happened. Before it did, Munna would sleep in the same room, lying on the floor with Kalipodo, while Chandona slept on the cot. He was known to everyone as Kalipodo's brother. Now, he had to sleep in the veranda.

It was about ten-thirty in the morning. Those who had come to the city on work were about to return, among them fishmongers, vegetable-sellers, and daily labourers who had not got any work today. Platform No. 2 was bursting at the seams. They would dive for the doors as soon as the down train entered.

Platform No. 1 was chock-a-block with men and women on their way to their offices. The train had started filling at every station until it was bulging with bodies. Still, everyone was desperate for a toehold. It wasn't just their jobs, people from the villages came to the city for court cases, medical treatment, meetings with ministers and bureaucrats, rallies and processions.

These crowded compartments were what Roton babu preferred. As everyone rushed to get in, Kalipodo would be right in front, and behind him the anxious masses. About to enter the compartment, Kalipodo would stop abruptly and shout, 'Let go of my slippers, let go.' If he could just hold up the passengers for a few moments, that was enough for Roton babu at the back of the crowd to pick up several wallets from pockets. Even ghaobaaji wasn't ruled out if needed. He was very quick; no one would find out.

This one time, he had used his ghaobaaji skills to pull out someone's wallet from their back pocket, but somehow the blade had nicked the victim's skin. He began to bleed, his white trousers turning red, but he had no idea.

Today, though, Ratan babu and his gang were not paying much attention to the office-bound passengers. Their best time was between the first and fifteenth of every month. It was the twentieth today. At best they'd get fifty or hundred and a monthly ticket in the wallet. It wouldn't even buy a hot meal for a family of four. And so, Ratan babu wasn't interested in them. He was on the lookout for a trader or middleman.

At about the same time, Sheikh Anwar the madari was gathering a crowd in the small expanse of open space in front of the rickshaw line outside Jadavpur Railway Station, performing quick magic tricks to attract an audience. Asking a labourer for his gamchha, he ripped it up into four pieces and then put them back together again before returning the whole gamchha. From another man he took a one-rupee coin and turned it into a ten-rupee one. Hypnotising an assistant with a chant, he made him lie down on the ground and then levitated him.

One trick followed another, and the audience began to swell. Finally, when the crowd was large enough, Sheikh Anwar started his real performance. First, he placed a beautiful bag on the chest of his assistant, who was lying on the ground. In the bag, he claimed, was a powerful amulet from the temples of Kamrup Kamakshya, an amulet that would bring triumph over enemies and victory in litigation, that would mesmerise women, secure profits in business, ensure jobs for the unemployed. Even acute illnesses would be cured. To put it simply, one amulet, a hundred benefits. And very cheap, too!

No one should take his word for it, of course—they should demand proof. And proof there was. Five or six people would materialise from the crowd and provide testimony of how the amulet had helped them. But this would take place a little later, for before that, a couple of other miracles would be wrought. The boy lying on the ground would be blindfolded with a piece of cloth folded over four times, and Anwar the magician would ask him some questions about things he shouldn't be able to see. He would answer them correctly with the power of the amulet, even though this was impossible when blindfolded.

One of the rickshaw-drivers here was named Modna, a union leader on this rickshaw line. The union here had been set up by hardcore leftists, who did not care for caste, destiny, or religion, who did not acknowledge the existence of gods. They said man had made god, not the other way round. And behind this claim lay logic, not emotion. Modna considered their reasoning sound—coming into contact with party leaders had turned him into an atheist, who was deeply sceptical of miracles and the supernatural. His own investigations had shown him that there was no truth in the reasons for which people believed in these things. It had been his idea to place the idol of Shitala beneath the banyan tree to prevent people from pissing there—no god-fearing person would have dared do it. It was because of the lessons on atheism that Modna had taken that the people of the area had been saved from the horrible stench.

One day, on his way back after dropping a passenger in Tollygunge, he had discovered a madari about to start a magic show on the road, and stopped to watch. The magician warned everyone before he began his performance, 'Anyone who wants to leave can leave right now—I won't stop you. But no one must leave in the middle of the performance, no one must move till I say so. I will make an enclosure here with a line on the ground, like Lakshman did for Sita maiya. Anyone who crosses the Lakshman Rekha and gets into trouble had better not blame me for it. I won't be responsible, I'm making it clear right now.'

Then he began his performance. Hypnotising an assistant, as Sheikh Anwar had done, he laid him on the ground and plunged a dagger into his throat. Everyone reacted in horror, one more than the rest. One onlooker said, 'I can't bear to see blood, my head is spinning, I have to go.'

Sternly the magician said, 'Do not get up. Stay where you are. I cannot save my brother if you cross the line.'

'I have to go,' the man moaned, 'I cannot take it anymore.' He rose to his feet. This time the magician roared even louder, 'Stay where you are.' Disobeying him, the man began to advance, but barely had he taken a few steps when the magician bellowed in anger, 'Stop!' The man could no longer move. The magician sat on the ground and brought his fist down on it. 'Come back!' And at once, amazingly, the man slumped to the ground, trembling, and proceeded to roll back to his previous position from a distance of twenty feet. The audience was dumbstruck. They burned and sweated beneath the midday sun but didn't dare move. The performance went on, and the collection of money continued. The magician issued an advance warning: 'Those who have nothing needn't give anything. But if those of you who do have money leave without donating for Ma Kamakshya, don't blame me if you find your pockets empty when you go home.'

A little later, another man got up and said, 'I have to go, I'll miss my train.' The magician forbade him too. 'Not now, a couple of minutes later, after my brother has recovered.' When ten minutes had passed, the man ignored the warning and began to walk off, whereupon he too collapsed to the ground at the magician's order and rolled back to his spot.

One person after another rose to leave at intervals and duly slumped to the ground, till the number had climbed to seven. A boy of twelve or thirteen, a babbling drunkard—they were all there.

Modna was not as troubled by the others as by the drunkard, who had done exactly what he himself would have—he had thrown a challenge to the magician. 'Tricks. Made up. Drama. All of them are your men. I know these things. I'm leaving. Let's see what you can do to me.' But hardly had he taken a few steps when he, too, collapsed, bleeding from the mouth.

Modna was taken aback by this horrifying scene. Was I wrong to believe what the party dadas told me? Were they mistaken even though they're educated? Do these incantations work after all? He was shaken to the core. But then he remembered what one of the party leaders had told him: 'Do not believe what you have not seen for yourself, do not believe what the teacher tells you.'

So Modna decided to test the magician for himself. What was the worst that could happen? He would fall to the ground. There was no one he knew in the crowd who would witness the humiliation, but it would be a small price to pay if it dispelled his scepticism. So he announced, 'I'm leaving, I cannot stay here any longer.' The magician stared at him, and then said, as sternly as usual, 'Didn't I already say no one must leave?' Modna was determined to test him. 'I'm going,' he said, 'stop me if you can.'

The magician looked helpless momentarily. The act couldn't be stopped just yet, many people had not yet paid up. But he gathered his wits quickly. 'Oh, you're a rickshaw-driver? I won't stop you then, you have to earn a living—I can't kick a poor man. Carry on.'

Modna was unhappy at this outcome. He went away a short distance, but he didn't leave. He had to find out who was telling the truth, the magician selling amulets, or the half-mad bearded men he knew.

When all the amulets had been sold, and money collected even from those who couldn't afford them, the magician and his companion gathered their things and set off. Modna followed them in his rickshaw. They walked a long way along the main street, and then entered a small park and lowered their bundles. Then they proceeded to count the currency notes and coins. Soon afterwards, the seven men who had slumped to the ground appeared one by one to collect their payments.

The drunkard was indeed drunk, his steps were still wavering. But he had played his role to perfection, earning himself not only his due payment but also a little extra money for another bottle. Now Modna understood, and his faith in logic was restored.

Which was why he was laughing to himself now as he watched Anwar perform in front of Jadavpur Station. But his mirth died when he spotted Roton and his gang in the crowd. Some members of the audience were going to have their pockets emptied out.

Meanwhile, the assistant who was lying on the ground blindfolded was listening carefully to the magician's questions, which contained hints that would lead him to the correct answer.

'Khoka!'

'Yes?'

'Where are you?'

'Here.'

'Where am I?'

'There.'

'Will you answer all my questions?'

'I will.'

'Are you sure?'

'Yes.'

'Khoka.'

'Yes?'

'Come here.'

'Here I am.'

'Go there.'

'Here I go.'

'Do you know that dada there?'

'I do.'

'Who is he?'

'She. A didi, not a dada.'

'No didi there.'

'Didi, not dada.'

The assistant was right. The audience marvelled at his ability. The gods were still powerful. Amulets could still exert their power. It was the Koli Jug, but so what?

'Khoka.'

'Yes?'

'Come here.'

'Here I am.'

'Go there.'

'Here I go.'

'Do you know this person?'

'I do.'

'Do you know what's in his heart?'

'I do.'

'Will you tell us about him?'

'I will.'

'Khoka.'

'Go there.'

'Here I go.'

'Who is this man?'

'It's not a man, it's a dog.'

Once again the audience marvelled at this. How did he know it's our mangy dog?

Having watched Anwar many times, Modna had cracked the code. Dada referred to a woman, man to a dog.

'Are you sure it's a dog?'

'Yes.'

'No, you're wrong.'

'It's a dog.'

'Do you know what colour?'

'I do.'

'Will you tell us its colour?'

'I will.'

'What colour is it?'

'Red.'

'No, it isn't red.'

The sequence of words in the question held the answer.

Modna had watched this performance day after day. He knew that some people claiming to have benefited from the amulets would now make their appearance. Some of them were rickshaw-drivers, some porters; even Bhola from the paanshop near the banyan tree was among them. They would claim to have been released from a case after being framed by the police, or to have recovered their rickshaw after it was lost, or to have increased their sales. And what would they get for telling these lies? A cup of tea, a piece of cheap cake wrapped in paper, a cigarette.

But Modna could now see Roton Mukherjee, Munna, Kalipodo and Chandona in the crowd, scanning them carefully. After all, behind the success of any operation was close observation.

Anwar's performance was in full swing now. Sleight of hand wasn't enough to enthrall the audience—the magician had to be a master of patter too. Anwar had the gift of the gab that enabled him to hoodwink everyone.

There was a human circle now around him and his assistant, most of them hardworking, poor people. But a handful among them had some money left over after buying their daily necessities. They were Anwar's targets.

Now he noticed Roton and his cohort mingling with the crowd. He knew at once what his task was—he had to warn his audience. Not doing this would be wrong of him.

So Anwar said, 'To all the dadas and didis and behens and babus here, I request you to enjoy my magic show. I won't ask anyone for money. You can spit on my hand if I do. So, enjoy the performance, but mind your pockets. There are some false babus here, waiting to make off with your money. Don't ask me for a receipt if they do. I can't give you one.'

He looked meaningfully at Roton babu, meaning, 'I've done my bit, now you do yours.' And Roton babu nodded back. 'Okay, boss, we have no quarrel between us.'

Both Roton and Anwar were aware of human psychology. They knew everyone would be careful now, and that extra caution sometimes served just the opposite purpose. Simultaneously with Anwar's warning, Roton, Munna, Chandona and Kalipodo's sharp eyes and restless hands were at work, examining pockets, waistbands and other parts of the body. Intent on guarding their money, those who had any provided unintended clues to its location.

In this way, the gang of four narrowed down the choice to a few targets.

'That fellow there. What do you think?'

'That old man?' came the answer. 'Nothing but small change.'

'What about that dhoor there?'

'Two dasu one pachu at most in his breast pocket. See the cement stains on his leg? Daily labourer. Assistant mason maybe. Didn't get work today, going back home. Twenty, twenty-five is all he has.'

'Looks like he has twenty-five thousand in there.'

'Twenty-five is like twenty-five thousand for him.'

Both were rejected, by society and by the gang of four. Another person kept feeling his hip pocket. The word went round. 'Might get something there. But two or three green ones at most. Not worth it.'

'The one next to him?'

'Looks like he might have three or four red Gandhis. Fishy smell. See his right elbow? That's a fish scale. This dhoor sells fish. Let's do him. Not now, after the show, when he's headed for the train. Grab him in the crowd at the gate and slit his pocket.'

'Will you be able to spot the fucker afterwards?' Roton asked his companions.

'No problem, ostad,' said Kalipodo. 'Half-sleeved blue shirt, black pants.'

'Let's go then. Tea-stall. A glass of water, some tea.'

'Tea in this weather?'

'I'm having some whether you do or not. Kill the heat with more heat.'

The ticket counter was on the left, the tea-stall on the right. Not many people travelling on this line bought tickets here. Likewise, hardly anyone bought a cup of tea from Montu-da's tea-stall. It wasn't so much tea as it was hot water. Anyone who worked here could learn how to make tea cheaply like Montu-da, with barely any tea leaves or sugar or milk. Rickshaw-drivers hereabouts said, 'Drinking tea at Montu-da's is like pouring money down the drain.' None of them frequented his stall, preferring to walk down to Bolai-da's, who added a little cream to every cup of tea he served. Such pleasure at the very first sip! A large tea and a hunk of bread at Bolai-da's was the usual mid-morning meal for most rickshaw-drivers. He sold omelettes and aluddom too. A half plate of aluddom meant a saucer brimming with curry and two pieces of potato. Eaten with bread, it was a full meal. But right now, Roton and his gang had no choice but to patronise Montu-da, so that they could keep an eye on the audience watching Anwar's show. They hadn't made any money since the morning. They would have to nail their quarry when he was about to enter the station. And if that didn't work, they would have to follow him as far as he went. Now that they had identified him as carrying a fat wad of cash, they couldn't let him go. He wouldn't be as alert after the show ended.

Roton asked for some tea, and so did everyone else. Roton Mukherjee had just taken his first sip of the bland, bitter liquid and raised his eyes, when his jaw dropped in surprise. The young man standing there on the platform, wasn't that Imaan? What was he doing here? When did he get out of jail? Roton remembered the old days. He had given the boy a pair of his trousers when he was released.

There was a clerk at the Alipur Court whose name was also Roton. All the tingbaajes in town were his client. He could get them released whether they could pay him on the spot or not. But being frequent offenders, they never cheated Clerk Roton. The one who stands by you at the crematorium and on the threshold of the court is your true friend. No one cheated a true friend like Clerk Roton. Who would save them the next time in that case?

Those who ended up in jail paid Clerk Roton with the money from their first theft after getting out. Some of those who were exonerated in court went off directly to the bus-stop to pick a pocket so that they could pay up immediately.

Roton Mukherjee had found himself in this situation once. He had no money to pay the clerk. He always had some money set aside for such expenses, but who was going to inform his wife to bring the money to the court?

That was the first time the two Rotons had met each other. Sent to the court from the police station, Roton Mukherjee would have gone to jail unless the bail money was provided. That was when a friend of his, who was involved in a much bigger case, had introduced them. 'Roton-da, meet my old friend, his name is Roton too. Honest fellow, always keeps his word. You know better than anyone else what the name means. He's been charged under 379. Get him out. He'll pay when he's free—he has money at home.'

IPC 379 meant the police suspected him of being involved in antisocial activities. No proof, only suspicion. Most pickpockets were charged under this section. Even if the accused could not pay for bail, the judge usually freed them after ninety days.

Clerk Roton couldn't turn the request down since he was handling the case of the person who had interceded on Roton Mukherjee's behalf. He had the pickpocket freed. As for Roton, master of his trade, the man with magnetic fingers, he didn't have to go home to pay the clerk; he collected the money on the street and went back immediately to settle his dues down to the last paisa. Since then, the two Rotons had been close friends.

When he was released from jail, Roton Mukherjee went to the clerk and said, 'I feel really bad for the boy, he's rotting in jail for no fault of his. Can't you have him released? I'll pay whatever it takes.

Clerk Roton said, 'There's nothing I can do. I could have had him released if he'd been a thief or a murderer. But he's innocent. It's as difficult to get an innocent person out of jail as it's easy to get a criminal out.' Pickpocket Roton knew this first-hand.

Now he called out to Imaan, 'Imaan, is that you? Come here. Remember me? Roton-da from ward no. 7.'

Imaan came up to him. 'Of course I do, dada. How can I forget you? You're one of the very few nice people I met in jail.'

'Never mind all that, when were you released?'

'Today. This morning.'

'What are you doing here?'

'I don't know where to go or what to do. I'm looking for somewhere to stay.'

'Who's that chhabal, Roton-da?' asked Chandona.

'Chhabal? Stop talking like a villager, you've lived in the city long enough now.'

'All right, all right, chhele. Who's the boy?'

'Oh it was a long time ago, none of you were working with me then. I'd chased a dhoor loaded with rokra to Gopalnagar. I was desperate. There was a policeman in plain clothes; he recognised me. Nabbed on the spot. My thekbaajes all ran away. No one knew where my house was, so they couldn't inform my wife.'

'How could they inform when you never let anyone know where you live,' Chandona interrupted.

'Never mind all that now. So there I was, out of my territory. Clerk Roton would have had me released if it was Alipur Court, but I was taken to Bankshall Court. I knew no one there, no one knew me either. So jail for three months. I was in file no. 7 at Central, bang opposite the chhokra file, two sides of the same railing. That's where I met him. Known him since then.'

'Yes, you said. Figured you knew him in jail from your question. What I'm asking is, is he in our line of work too?'

'Oh! no, no, no,' Roton protested vehemently. 'He's a good boy.'

'Oh, and we're not good?'

'Of course not. All of you are good too. But he's good in a different way.'

'Then why was he in jail?'

'No time for that story now, I'll tell you later. Pathetic ... A path ... pathe ... pathetic story.'

Roton turned to Imaan and said, 'So you've been released at last. Remember how you used to say you'd never be free? Now you are.'

'I am, but now I wish I wasn't,' Imaan said. 'I have no idea where to live, what to do. If I'd been in jail, by now I'd have ...' He wanted to add, '... got a hot meal.' His stomach was churning with hunger, but he couldn't bring himself to say it. What use would it be anyway. As his friend Komol had said in jail, 'They'll be jealous of your joys, they'll laugh at your suffering. The rules outside are different. It's not like jail. The less you speak of yourself the better.'

But Roton seemed to have got it although Imaan hadn't spoken. 'Look,' he said, 'jail is jail, and the outside is the outside. You won't get here what you get there, and what you get here you won't get there. You'll have to look for things you can do. And as for where to live ...' Roton paused before continuing, 'that's not a problem at all. Make enough rokra and you can hire a room. By the hour, by the month, by the year. You can hire a wife, too, and you can live happily with her. But no notes, no votes. Thousands of *haate-khola-pode-mala* paupers here. God has given them the gift of the railway platform. Hundreds live here. They're born here, they grow up here—they even have families here. You can live like them, with them, if you like. But yes, it's true no one will serve you a hot meal at the right time like they did in jail. You have to make your own arrangements for food. I was as helpless as you are when I came to Calcutta for the first time. You know what I used to do? I'd eat at a bhaater hoteyl and run away without paying. Then I learnt things on my own. And now look, I run my own life, my family, and even the gang's household. I could add you to the gang, but I won't. I don't want you to have to go back to jail. It's different for us, we can spend a month there and a month here. What I suggest is, why don't you work at One-Armed Paanu's scrapyard for now. He'll hire you if I tell him. Afterwards, you can figure out something better.'

'Scrapyard. But even their work is illegal. The police arrest them sometimes—I've met them in jail.'

'That's true,' Roton nodded. 'In that case, why don't you become a ragpicker. Collect scraps and sell them. No need to be anyone's fucking servant. You're your own boss. Do your rounds, take your stuff to Paanu, collect your cash, buy a meal, spread your gamchha on the platform and go to sleep. No one will bother you if you don't cheat them.'

The reference to the gamchha reminded Imaan he hadn't bathed today. At this hour yesterday, he was trying to catch a post-lunch nap. That was what his friends must be doing now, because they were in jail, and the state was taking care of them. But now that he had been set free, Imaan was responsible for himself. He was free not to bathe, he was free not to eat and lie down beneath a tree, he was free to make a noose and hang himself. These were the benefits of freedom.

'Then what should I do now, dada?' asked Imaan.

'What should you do? Wait here at the station. Paanu's scrapyard is closed now, it'll open later in the afternoon. I'll take you there, get you to talk to him, and arrange for a sack for you.'

Roton paused to look at Anwar's audience and leapt in the air. 'Where's the dhoor gone, Chandona? Blue shirt-black pants?'

No one had been paying attention, allowing their quarry to escape. What now?

'Suck your bloody fingers now, that's what,' said Roton in a fury. 'Not one fucking job can you arseholes do properly. You'll see when I'm arrested. All you baanchots will have to beg on the platform. Go fuck yourselves—it's pack-up today.'

One of Roton's assets was his ability to calm down as quickly as he flared up. It happened this time too. A minute ago, he was snarling. But now, on spotting Beji approaching from a distance, he said gently, 'Ei Beji.'

'What is it, Roton-da?'

'Where are you going?'

'Hospital pond. Need to bathe. Dying of heat.'

Roton hadn't asked, but Beji revealed his subsequent plans too. 'After the bath, the university. Chhatu with green chillies and chaatni outside the gate. Then back to the hospital. Nap beneath the tree till the sun goes down. After that, I'll see.'

Beji was awfully sad today. The kind of sadness that couldn't be shared with anyone. Now he was trying to dismiss his suffering with a snap of his fingers.

Pointing to Imaan, Roton said, 'Take him with you. My son. I'm entrusting him to you. Look after him. He's innocent, doesn't know anything. Make sure he's with you all the time. Give him some chhatu too. Then take him to Paanu later. I'll talk to Paanu. All right?'

'Give him chhatu?' Beji mumbled. 'But I ...' Before he could finish, Roton handed him a fifty-rupee note. 'Any other problem?'

'None.'

6

It was summer when Aamodi's husband Jongol Poramanik had died. The trees, the earth, the people were all being scorched by the merciless heat at the time. Almost three months had passed since then. Summer had given way to the monsoon, and the rains were also proving abnormal this year. There was water overflowing everywhere, in drains and canals, lanes and alleys. But although the season had changed, Aamodi's situation had not. She had been suffering from insomnia for three months. Ever since Jongol's death, she had not slept well at night. The house seemed empty, and she felt lonely and bereft. Whatever his faults, her husband's presence had been a source of confidence for her. People treated her with respect—she had a man back home, who could at least shout loudly even if he couldn't move.

A man at home and a scarecrow in the field are equally useful. They can do something even when they cannot do anything. 'Don't lie there like a corpse, keep an eye on things. I'm going to the handpump for a drink of water. Not a drop at home, what will I pour into your mouth when you die.' She could talk to him when there was no one else to talk to. She could swear at him when there was no one else to swear at.

Aamodi's husband was gone now, Aamodi was up for grabs. The word went round, and once it did, no one respected her anymore. Like flies buzzing around ripe fruit, men hovered around Aamodi's hut late at night, alone or in pairs, whispering, chuckling. Aamodi could tell their voices and footsteps apart. Some came in rubber slippers and some, in plastic shoes, leaving footprints in the wet soil, signs that they had been impatiently circling her house. Which was why Aamodi felt afraid as the night deepened, shrinking back in fear in the pitch dark interior of her hut. Sex was for pleasure, but rape was horrifying—and gang rape? She had seen the dead body of a raped woman in a goods train carriage. Scratches and bites all over her naked body, clotted blood leading back to her mauled vagina. A gang of beasts had attacked her, raping her through the night before abandoning her, half-dead, in the goods train, where she had died. The memory was terrifying.

Ponchu Nayek's widow Shudashibala lived next door. One day, Aamodi confided her fears to her. 'Some people walk around my house late at night and say things. My heart quakes in fear. They could break in any night—what if they do? They'll tear me apart like a dog.'

Shudashi paid no attention to Aamodi. You're a widow of three or four months, I've been a widow for two years. People circle your house, don't I live in a house too? I don't hear anything. At least you have a door, I don't even have one, only a sheet. Wouldn't someone have come in by now? Drama! People skulking around my house. Meaning what?

Meaning, see, I have a market. Now that I'm available, men are lining up. You think I don't get it. I was born the year of the flood, I know what you'll say before you say it. Don't try your tricks with me!

Aamodi shared her fears with one or two others as well. They worked like dogs all day, and fell on their beds like the dead after they had eaten. None of them had ever heard footsteps. Like the atheist who refuses to believe in God, no one in the slum was ready to accept the existence of these creatures of the night.

A man named Pobon said, 'I can swear it's not a human. We'd have known otherwise—we live next door. My sixth sense tells me it's Jongol's spirit. That's why only you can see him. You didn't do the rites properly, didn't get a priest. His soul hasn't been released. It's hovering around here in rage and sorrow. Hasn't harmed you yet, but who knows, might do something any day. You can't trust spirits. What I say is, even if you have to borrow the money, go to Kalighat and do the rituals.'

Inevitably, news of Jongol Poramanik's soul not having found release and roaming around the slum spread everywhere. A few days later, some woman out for a piss by the railway lines in the clear moonlight after a shower saw Jongol perched on the branch of the guava tree outside Aamodi's hut, swinging his legs and smoking. She was so frightened she couldn't make it as far as the tracks, and peed in her sari at once. Unable to speak in fear, she managed to run back home, bolt her door and collapse to the floor, almost unconscious. Bhorot the baul came to investigate, and found her testimony more convincing than Aamodi's.

Not the doing of humans, it was clearly the work of a dissatisfied spirit.

'Jongol keeps coming back because of his wife and child. I saw for myself how hard he had worked to build this house—how can anyone let go so easily? My view is, go to Kalighat and do his rites the proper way. It'll cost about a hundred. I'll lend it to you. Return it whenever you want. I'll lower the interest—just five rupees a day. Just give me the five every morning, you can pay back the principal later. Everything will be fine once you do the rites at Kalighat.'

Moharaj, who lived two houses down from Aamodi, was not willing to believe in ghosts and spirits. 'We never stand by one another in times of trouble,' he said. 'That's why things are getting out of hand. Bad characters are trying to get their hands on the women here. The whole thing will stop if we stay up a few nights, catch this fellow and beat him up. No spirit will show up after that.'

Someone replied, 'Who's going to beat whom up, Moharaj-da? Everyone has shit in their arses—no one's a saint. If people have to be beaten up, no one can be spared. A ghost will be found in every house, from the first one to the last.'

The first one! Moharaj knew what the man was getting at. The way he was pointing made it obvious. The very first house on entering this lane was Moharaj's. Many of his neighbours didn't like Shorongi babu frequenting his house. This was clearly what the speaker was hinting at. Moharaj was overcome by a feeling of inadequacy. He was at a loss for words. His head slumped, he condemned himself. He was furious with Ranibala, but he simply couldn't get himself to take it up with her. The news of what Ranibala had been up to would blow in on the wind when he was in jail. He had vowed that his first task on getting out would be to choke his adulterous wife to death with a pillow.

Moharaj may well have done just that, had he not met Shonkor Bag shortly before he was to be released. Shonkor had been convicted in a case of murder and robbery. He could have been given the death sentence, only luck had saved him, so that he had been sentenced for life instead. In jail this was referred to as 'beesh shaal', and the convict, as a 'beesh shaalia'. But if a beesh shaalia could spend fourteen years quietly and in a civil manner, without getting into trouble or fights, without having more cases slapped on them, there was a possibility of an early release. Shonkor had chosen to cooperate, and was counting the days to be free again.

When he went to jail, he had left his young wife outside. She had given birth to two children in five years, which had made Shonkor the butt of many jokes in prison.

'Do you know magic, Shonkor? Do you turn yourself into a bird and fly away every night and come back in the morning?'

'I don't understand,' Shonkor had said in surprise.

'You're in jail and your wife's having babies every year. What's going on?'

Shonkor was incensed by the taunts, but there was nothing he could do, because the bitter truth had to be acknowledged. He was furious with his wife. He was a 'med' in the prison, which meant he was allowed to be in plain clothes and wear a brass belt. Meds were the most respected jail members after the guards there. But now, his wife had robbed him of his stature. That's why he was angry. How could she be such a fool! The government distributed contraceptive pills free of cost—why couldn't she take them? My prestige would have remained intact.

One day, Shonkor had opened his heart to Moharaj. 'At first, I thought I'd kill her when I got out of jail. Now I tell myself it's my fault. I married her. I'm responsible for her food and clothing. But I couldn't provide for her, so what was she to do? Hunger makes you desperate. I killed a man for it. The man had been married for just a month. I was about to grab his wife's jewellery, but he thought I was going to rape her. Lost his head and attacked me with an axe. What could I do? I had to fire my pipe gun in self-defence. The bullet went straight into his chest. I ate up an entire family. But my wife, she's not doing any harm to anyone else; she's allowing vultures to eat her instead. I can't blame her—let her survive any way she can.'

As Shonkor started weeping, his tears softened Moharaj, too, who changed his mind. He realised why Ranibala had done what she had, and said to himself, 'I forgive you, Rani, it's not your fault, it's mine. Forgive me.'

But even if Moharaj had forgiven his wife, his neighbours were unwilling to forgive him. They made their disapproval clear with sneers and jeers. Earlier it was behind his back, but now they told him on his face. Rani and Moharaj had quarrelled about this. He had said, 'Never mind what happened earlier, tell Shaadhin babu not to come here anymore. People talk—I can't take it.'

'Then don't,' Ranibala had snapped back. 'Who's asking you to listen? Stuff your ears with cotton. The man's done so much for us, built us a proper home. Who else in the bosti has brick walls? Who pays for our food and clothes? Are you capable of supporting a wife? Your arse will shrivel into a raisin if he doesn't give us money for even a month! People talk because they have mouths to talk with, what do I care? Do they support me? Will any of them come forward if we run out of food tomorrow? Why do you stay here if it troubles you so much? Walk to the station and take a train to wherever the fuck you want to go, where no one knows you.'

Rani's barbs had stung that day. Now, this man's mocking tongue was slicing him up. Moharaj felt like a dead man, cremated on a pyre, rejected, mere scrap.

The man who had humiliated him had no idea that he had lit a fire. Soon after this conversation, Shibpodo returned from the potato godown to the slum. Hearing that his beloved Aamodi boudi was feeling threatened, he postponed his bath and lunch and rushed to her house covered in grime, sweat and rain. 'What's all this I hear?' he said. 'Someone's got his eyes on you? You're going to find it hard to protect yourself, this door of yours can be opened with one push. What if someone gets in at night and does something to you?'

'You'll have to come at once,' said Aamodi. 'A case will have to be filed with the police, he'll have to be made to go to jail.'

Shibpodo was a little flustered at the mention of the police and jail. 'Of course,' he said, 'but will it restore your honour?'

'I understand what you're saying, thakurpo,' Aamodi said with a worried look, 'but what should I do? Where will I go if I leave the bosti?'

Knowing what the men in the slum thought of women, Shibpodo said apprehensively, 'Where can you go, boudi? It's the same everywhere.'

'I could go across the river to Sodorbon,' said Aamodi. 'I have relatives there.'

'What will you do there, how will you support yourself? You have a son, he has to go to school, he has to be brought up properly. Without an education he'll end up like us, driving a rickshaw or working as a labourer. Bhubon and I grew up together, but because he went to school till class eight, he got a corporation job. Two hours of cleaning drains every day, no other work, full pay. I have to fucking start in the morning, and this is the time I get back. Then again from the afternoon till nine or ten at night. Call this a life?'

'It's the boy I worry for,' said Aamodi. 'Else, just feeding myself wouldn't be such a problem. I could just get a job as a maid, easy work—and money at the end of the month.'

'That's what I say too. Don't think of leaving. Why should you leave your own home? If you go away, it might be to a big house, but it'll be someone else's.'

Aamodi smiled with her eyes. 'That's all very well, but what if someone breaks in, like you said?'

Shibpodo had been trying to make use of the lull between the sounds of passing trains, attempting to convey the unsaid to Aamodi. Now, taking a deep breath, he finally came out with it. 'Tell you something, boudi?'

'Yes, I want to hear what you have to say.'

'You won't mind, no?'

'I won't.'

'You won't tell anyone?'

'I won't. Tell me.'

'What I say is, if you're frightened here, sleep in my house. You can spend the day in your own home. Nothing to worry about by daylight. I have a large bed, four of us can fit in easily. Two grown-ups, two children, no problem. And if you don't want to do that ...'

'And if I don't want to do that?'

'Then I can spend the night in your house. I can sleep in a corner.'

Aamodi chuckled. 'I used to think you're a fool. Now I see you're just the opposite.'

Boudi isn't angry! I've managed to say it. She's understood. Shibpodo savoured her praise. In a gratified voice, he said, 'What are you saying! Everyone says I'm ...'

'They don't know you yet, that's why they think you're a fool.' After a pause, Aamodi continued, 'Tell me, thakurpo, suppose there's a boti on the floor and I drop a laau on its blade. What will happen?'

'The laau will be sliced into two pieces.'

'And suppose the laau is on the floor and I drop the boti on it?'

'Same thing. The laau will be sliced into two pieces.'

Looking Shibpodo in the eye, Aamodi said, 'So, laau on boti or boti on laau—it's the laau that will be sliced into two pieces. Whether I sleep in your house or you sleep in mine, who will be harmed?'

'Harm? What harm? I said I'd sleep as far away from you as possible.'

'Who's going to check in the darkness how far away you are. It's my reputation that'll be destroyed.' Aamodi paused for a few moments. 'Not that that's what I'm worrying about. Who can ruin reputations here, who has a reputation in the first place? Bitch goes to bed with another man while her bhaatar keeps watch at the door. If that doesn't ruin her reputation, what can anyone do to me? Whores with husbands at home sleep with a dozen men. I don't even have one. Am I an old woman? Don't I have needs? But that's not what I'm thinking of. I'm thinking, you never know what the heart demands. Suppose you roll towards me and I don't push you away, or I roll towards you and you don't push me away—what will happen then?'

'What will happen?'

'That's what I'm saying, what will happen? What if a baby is made?'

'Nothing will happen,' Shibpodo said resolutely.

This infuriated Aamodi. 'What will not happen? I won't get pregnant?'

'No no no, that's not what I'm saying.'

'Then what will not happen? You'll stay away? Are you a hermit? A locked-down nagababa, who doesn't turn the key even when a woman's within reach? I've seen hundreds of hermits like you who can control themselves. You think you can? You have so much power? The holiest of men lose their heads, who the fuck are you? Do you know what the sound of raindrops on a tin roof is like? Do you know what it does to the body? Never mind you, not even someone sworn to celibacy can hold themselves back.'

'Not saying that,' Shibpodo mumbled. 'I'm saying there's one thing we can do to make sure there's no harm.'

'What's that?'

'You get this balloon kind of thing in shops. They distribute them free in the villages, it has a name—Nirodh. Using one of those means no children.'

'I don't like balloons inside me,' Aamodi said after a pause. I might as well get a candle then—she told herself—who needs a man.

'There's another way out too,' Shibpodo said.

'Which is?' said Aamodi, glumly.

'Get an operation. Beshpoti's wife, Netto's wife, Shudashi, they've all done it. Now they can do what they like—it's safe.'

Aamodi grew livid. Beads of perspiration gathered on her forehead. In a murderous voice, she said, '*I'll* have the operation, *my* blood will flow, the pain will all be *mine*. Why? I support myself, I'm not asking for your money. Not asking for sidoor either. What do you have to do then? You won't take any responsibility, you'll only share my bed?'

Taken aback, Shibpodo groped in vain for a response.

'If I get an operation,' Aamodi continued, 'why should my door be open only to you? Which kingdom are you the crown prince of? Hundreds of better looking men out there. It's not like I don't know who circles my hut at night. If I call out, he'll crawl in.'

Shibpodo's dream was slipping out of his grasp. 'What should I do then, what do you suggest I do?'

'*You* get an operation,' Aamodi said. 'Can you do it? I'm scared of going under the knife. The doctor operated on me when my Giril was born. You'll see when I show you—they sliced my belly open. Eighteen stitches all the way down to my cunt. Can't do it again.'

There was a man named Bheem who worked with Shibpodo at the godown. His job was to deliver potatoes to shops in a rickshaw trailer. Bheem's formidable appearance matched his name. He used to single-handedly ferry twenty sacks of potatoes. But after three daughters in a row, he didn't want to risk having more children for the sake of a son, and decided to get an operation on his wife's advice. No one knew what happened after that, but Bheem began to wither away, and soon became a shadow of his former self. He could no longer work as hard as before, saying he felt palpitations and was out of breath easily. 'I feel weak, I've made a big mistake, I'll have to live like a sick man now. Anyone who listens to a woman dies before his lifespan ends. There's no joy in eating, no peace in sleeping, no pleasure even in the reason for doing this. I can't even do it anymore.'

If the body itself gives way, Shibpodo told himself, what's Aamodi boudi or the potato godown or this beautiful world any good for? The very reason for doing it would become meaningless. He shook his head. 'I can't do that.'

Aamodi was silent. Then she said in disappointment, 'That's that, then. You can go, it's no use hanging out here. And let me tell you before you go, if you spot the ghost who comes here at night, tell him I have a bottle of acid at home. If he tries to get into my house, he'll know what I'm like. I sleep with an axe by my side. First I'll fling the acid at him, then I'll lift his lungi and strike at his root. That cock for which he's putting in so much effort will become useless.'

Does Aamodi boudi suspect me then? Why is she saying this to me? I'm the one in a lungi—why did she say lungi and not pants?

Shibpodo realised he was tingling with fear now. The guava tree in front of Aamodi's house was swaying mockingly at him. No, the ghost wouldn't climb that tree anymore, nor circle Aamodi's house. What was the use? The honey was safely in the jar, out of reach. The fly would only have its heart broken.

7

Broken, deflated and disconsolate, Shibpodo gazed down the path along which he would return. He was full of expectations when he had walked up this way earlier, but now there was nothing but emptiness in his heart. A long cherished desire had evaporated in an instant. For three months he had waited to tell Aamodi boudi what he wanted, but the response was just another word for death. At least his days used to pass in hope earlier ... how would he bear the burden of life now?

'I'll go, then.' Shibpodo felt he was saying goodbye for the last time, that he would never return.

'Go,' said Aamodi disdainfully.

Still Shibpodo couldn't stir. But suddenly there was an uproar from somewhere near the railway line. A train was passing towards Garia, blowing its whistle. Some people were seen running towards the tracks, accompanied by Ranibala's wails. 'O Ram-er baap, ogo Baloram-er baap, what have you done, where have you gone leaving this wretched woman behind!'

Moharaj had gone? Gone where? Shibpodo could remain sitting no longer. He ran up to the railway lines to find

Moharaj's body lying across them, severed into two halves. Being run over by a train does not cause much bloodshed, for the wheels mutilate the body, so that the veins and arteries stop working. A little blood was still oozing from the sections near the waist. Moharaj's eyes were open, as though taking in a last glimpse of the beauty of the world. His eyelids and his severed body were trembling slightly; it would take some time for this to stop.

Most of the residents of the slum were away right now on work. Those who were at home came running out hearing Ranibala's shrieks. How had something so terrible happened?

Beji was in Moharaj's house at the time. He had dropped by to smoke some ganja. The whole thing had happened in full view. 'Moyaraj-da and I were smoking,' he said. 'His face didn't give away anything. A train was approaching. Moyaraj-da went out. I thought he was going for a piss. But he had other plans. When the train was nearby, he jumped into its path. It cut him into two pieces. Right in front of my eyes. Didn't give me time to stop him.'

'Why did he do it? Did he quarrel with his wife?'

'Not while I was there. Don't know what happened earlier. Rani-di was cooking. I could smell loittya. Moyaraj-da was making the smoke. Shibpodo and Aamodi were talking there. That's when it happened.'

A crowd had gathered by now. Polashi and Kamini were on their way for a bath, like always. They stopped here now. Monkhushi the mad woman was here too with her baby. She was crying as though someone of her own had died.

Gogon, Bhegai and Bishnu appeared too. One of them said to the other two, 'Moharaj-da honestly was always a gandu. Look at how he died. Will his body be of any use now? If you're going to die, do it in a way that helps others. Couldn't live properly, couldn't die properly either.'

Someone else said, 'The fucker didn't even put on his underwear. Bums balls all visible.'

Yet another person said, 'Cover those things with his lungi. Women are passing by.'

A response came from the crowd, 'No one's touching the dead body now. Police case, going to be trouble.'

Ranibala was weeping. Real tears. 'You wanted chicken, you son of a bitch, I went to the market to get it for you. You said, make it spicy, so I did. You said, haven't had loittya in a long time—I cooked that too. What am I going to do with that shit now? Couldn't you have stuffed your face before dying, you son of a whore.'

Everyone sympathised with Ranibala, everyone shared her grief. Someone said, 'Don't anyone tell the police it was suicide. Everyone say he desperately needed to shit and was running towards the trees across the tracks, didn't pay attention. Put a mug of water next to the body, it'll prove he was going for a shit. Otherwise, the police will create trouble, ask for lots of money.'

Moharaj had died. The manner of his death was a waste. A selfish man all his life, he hadn't forsaken his selfishness even in dying. You have a wife, two children—couldn't you think of them at least? What harm would it have done to die in a way that would have allowed them to get some money?

Thoroughly disappointed, Gogon, Bhegai and Bishnu realised that there was no point loitering here. So they headed back. 'We're going,' Bishnu said, 'the station master needs to be informed.' He would ring for the dom to come and dispose of the body. No one else could do it, considering the way Moharaj had died.

Twenty-five or so people were gathered around the corpse. Remarks flew around, as did the rancid smell of blood. Imaan joined the crowd now. Kamini nudged Polashi, 'There he is, that beimaan.'

'No, don't use that name. I'll start using it too and so will everyone else—it'll stick. It's not fair. He hasn't betrayed anyone.'

'Oh, such a soft heart,' Kamini sneered. 'What's wrong if it becomes his name, what do you and I care?'

Polashi said wistfully, 'If you can't help anyone, don't do them any harm either. A good person ought to have a nice name.'

'Oh, a good person? What kind of good? Sour or sweet? Tasted yet?'

'This isn't the time for jokes,' Polashi admonished Kamini lightly. 'Moharaj-da is dead, and here you are, making bad jokes next to his dead body. No sense at all, no idea whatsoever of time and place. You're not young anymore, when will you learn.'

Kamini felt like she had been hit by a sledgehammer. Polashi was talking of her age. Not young anymore. How much older am I than you? You're the one who's probably three or four years older, in fact. Just that you look better. Huh! If it weren't for the pill, Polashi would have had three or four children by now. Fucking whore! In her head, Kamini heaped abuse on Polashi.

Beji had been rooted to the spot from the beginning. He was the first witness of Moharaj's death. But he wouldn't stay any longer. What was the point of staring at a dead body? Besides, he needed a bath. He had come prepared for one, only stopping for a quick smoke before taking the road through Loharpara to the pond next to the hospital. He meant to have a meal of egg curry and rice at Chhechan-da's hoteyl afterwards.

He had a cake of fragrant soap, an expensive purchase. Half a day's income had gone into it. He had spotted Polashi and Kamini. Beji had learnt the game a few years ago, flashing the sunlight into someone's eye with a mirror. Now he turned the shiny wrapper of the soap into a reflecting surface, and flashed a beam into Kamini's eyes. Polashi's eyes were more beautiful, but they no longer drew Beji as before. There was no love or kindness in them.

It took Beji two or three attempts. Kamini laughed, happiness glinting in her eyes.

She went up to Beji. 'Did you buy that soap?'

'Obviously,' said Beji. 'The shopkeeper isn't my father-in-law. Won't give it to me free.'

'Such a lovely fragrance. How much did it cost?'

'A lot. You can't afford it.'

'Tell me anyway.'

'Why do you need to know? Want to use it? You can.'

Everyone has a weakness, Kamini's was soap. Both her heart and body felt fulfilled when she could bathe for an hour with an abundance of soap. She used a one-rupee bar of 501 every day, and her one luxury was to put on a clean sari after bathing. It was over her use of soap that she had fought with her Bihari husband. 'Who's going to pay for your soap every day?'

She had had an argument bordering on a quarrel with Polashi, too, yesterday. 'You use my soap every day ... you know how much it costs. You never stop once you start. Why can't you buy your own?'

'Did you say I use your soap every day? As if you don't use mine.'

'You call that soap? What you bring is a brick. Scrapes the skin off.'

'Mine is a brick and yours is butter? It's our own soap from tomorrow. No need to use each other's.'

It was a short exchange, but there was resentment concealed in it, which may not have been related to the soap alone. Beji, who was present, had no trouble understanding this. He had also realised that a simple cake of soap might allow him to get intimate with Kamini. He could puncture Polashi's pride by showing her he wasn't insignificant, that someone else valued him even if she didn't. Hence the expensive, fragrant soap bought from half a day's earnings.

Now that Kamini had seen the soap, she was impatient. 'When are you going for your bath?' she asked.

'That's what I came out for. But Moyaraj-da ...'

'It's all over here, what more is there to stare at. The dom will do the rest. Let's go to the pond.'

Then, making sure Polashi could hear, Kamini continued, 'Let's go to the ghat near the morgue. Fewer people there. Rub my back with the soap, Beji, all right? I can't reach properly. I'll rub yours too.' Her eyes were twinkling.

'I will.'

'Will what?'

Beji said innocently, 'Soap your back. Like you said.'

'Soapy hands are slippery. Are you sure they won't slip somewhere else?'

Polashi grimaced. A man was lying dead in full view of everyone. Ranibala's wails hung heavy in the air. There was grief everywhere. And these two were flirting. What was the source of all this rapture?

Kamini rolled her eyes to arouse Beji further. 'You could have said, will that be my fault, it'll be the fault of the hands.'

Going closer to him, she softened her voice. 'Ever touched a woman's body?'

Beji shook his head.

'Come, I'll let you touch mine today. Moharaj has died. No one can control death. At least you won't have any regrets if you die tomorrow.'

Kamini turned to Polashi. 'Are you coming, you bitch? Or do you want to feast your eyes on Moharaj's arse some more?'

'Go where?' Polashi was fuming.

'Where we are going. To bathe.'

'Let the dom take Moharaj-da away. Afterwards.'

'Stay here then, I'm going. Come, Beji.' Kamini strode off towards the pond. Throwing a glance at Polashi, Beji followed her.

8

A lane ran southwards on the other side of the railway lines. No, it wasn't exactly a lane, it was broader, wide enough for rickshaws, cycles and motorbikes. It led to an area named Loharpara, directly behind the hospital. Bagharmor could be reached through Loharpara, to the right of which, after a bend in the road, lay KPC Hospital.

The pond was next to the sweepers' quarters behind the hospital. It was large, almost a lake, with some greenery having survived around it. However, the trees would be cut down soon, for the hospital was being expanded after a change of ownership. Their future was uncertain, therefore.

But since they were still standing, there was a pleasantly magical greenish shadow over the area. Clouds had hidden the sun for a while, creating the illusion of dusk. Guaranteed to make the heart flutter.

The water in the pond wasn't clear; it had a greenish hue. The babu class never used it; they didn't lack for water, after all. There was an unlimited supply of water in the staff quarters. Those who bathed and washed their clothes in the pond did it only because they had no choice.

And so, the porters and labourers and rickshaw-drivers, men and women from the rail bosti, had got hold of bricks to construct a flight of stairs—a ghat they could use. It was not only well-built but also beautiful, which was why there was always a large crowd here. There was another ghat, too, near the shacks, occupied by the relatives of those who worked at the hospital—sons, brothers, cousins—who had nowhere else to live. They worked elsewhere in the city. These residents had built a few pigsties for extra income, selling—and sometimes eating—pork during festivals. They had built this particular ghat for their own requirements, using it to, among other things, collect water for their pigs. Here there were not only tall trees but also a dense wood, home to the ruins of an old morgue, piled high with torn quilts and mattresses. Not many people took the trouble to use this ghat because it needed an entire circuit of the pond to get to it. It was a matter of just a couple of dips, after all—who was going to walk so far.

It was to this safe, deserted ghat that Kamini and Beji had come today. Squatting on the ground, Beji said, 'Have you and Polashi quarrelled?'

'No. Why?'

'Looked that way. You just left her there. So I thought. You don't usually abandon each other.' Beji smiled. 'You run away from your bhaatars. She doesn't marry. People call you maag-bhaatar, husband and wife.'

'Which fuckface says this?' Kamini laughed.

'No, just that girls do marry each other these days. And boys marry boys. Can't blame anyone. People might think that way seeing the two of you.'

'Not really,' Kamini said candidly. 'Doesn't work for me. Tried it once or twice—you can't replace honey with sugar.'

'Still, she seemed upset you left her behind.'

Suddenly Kamini lost her head at Polashi being included in their intimate exchanges. 'Let her be upset,' she said furiously, 'what the fuck do I care!'

'You're friends after all.'

'What do you mean friends? We scavenge together, sell at the same place, live in the same bosti, that's all. I spent not even seven months with the men I vowed to spend my entire life with. This one's a friend only in name. Does she know what friendship is? Does she understand how to protect a friend?'

Beji was surprised to hear Kamini being so harsh about Polashi.

Kamini continued after a pause, 'People blame me for leaving my bhaatars. But it never starts with me. I just take revenge for what they do to me. If I think of living with someone else, he starts bullying me. So I throw him away like a torn slipper. In the morning I don't think twice about kicking away the man whose breast I slept on at night. Who's your Polashi in comparison?'

'What's your heart made of, Kamini?' asked Beji. 'Doesn't it hurt to leave someone you gave everything to? Someone you took everything from? Doesn't it matter?'

'Why must it matter?' Kamini said hotly. 'Don't you drink your tea and throw the cup away? Then why can't we? You think you're fucking lords because you're men? And we're nothing? What have you got that we haven't? Just that tiny wobbling leather pipe under that lungi—does that give you lot the right to do anything? Those days are gone. Women can do everything that men can. Want my respect? Better give me respect. Want to feel valued? Value me first. Give me love, you'll get love back. I'll give you double of everything you give me.'

Kamini was fuming. Beji understood she was enraged, but not the reason for it. Just a few minutes ago, she had been all over him. Where was that flirtatious figure now?

But Kamini seemed calmer after setting her clothes down on the ground and cleaning her teeth. She said, 'I've seen much more of the world than you have, dealt with many more people. Life has taught me a lot, things I'd never have learnt if I hadn't left home. I can tell you something now that will help you later. Should I?'

'Tell me. Anything you want.'

Kamini continued somewhat philosophically, 'Man or woman, a human is a human. You know what the human heart is like? It's like this pond. When you sit here on the ghat, your reflection will appear in the water. When you're gone, so's your reflection. Instead of you, the water now reflects whoever's sitting in your place. A day goes by, two days, a month. Then one day, you think of going back to see if your reflection's still there. You sit down, and there it is. It's the same with anyone who goes there, not just you.'

'You may think that way,' argued Beji. 'But not everyone does. The human heart and the water in the pond—what's the connection? Everyone is unique. So is their heart.'

Chewing on a blade of grass, he went on, 'You alone know what's in your heart. It's the same with me. You say the heart is like water. I say my heart is like a rock. The name that's been carved on it once can never be erased.'

Kamini looked daggers at him. 'Really? So it's Polashi.'

'What?'

'Polashi's name is carved on your rock. Never to be erased. But she writes a new name in the morning, wipes it out in the evening. Writes another one at night, wipes it out again. Your name's vanished by now—what about that? Will you just knock your head on that rock all your life and weep?'

'I know that,' said Beji ruefully. 'I know everything. You don't have to tell me. I've seen what she does. Not once, many times.' He choked, his eyes filled with tears. 'Still. Can't forget her. Can't hate her. Can't give her up.'

His sigh stung Kamini. Harshly she said, 'Break the rock if you want to survive. Or you'll be lying where Moharaj-da was today.'

Diving into the water, she swam some distance away before returning. Hauling herself out of the pond, she sat with her feet immersed in the water and smiled invitingly. 'Pass the soap,' she said.

When Beji handed it to her, she continued with the same smile, 'Over twenty, and you haven't touched a woman. Want to? Come to me. Soap my back.' Kamini raised her arms to untie her hair. Beji found it hard to control himself, and she sensed his eyes on her back. She knew she could reel the fish in.

'What are you staring at?' Kamini was a snake charmer now.

'Kamini.'

'Mmm.'

'There's something I want to say.'

'Say it, sonnabitch.'

'Suppose you ...'

'Suppose I ...'

'Suppose you were Polashi.'

'Polashi again!'

'No, just saying. If you were ...'

'Never,' Kamini screeched. 'I'll never be her. If I do anything, it will be after marriage. Not like her. Get into bed with anyone who asks. I've never done it. I'll have a proper wedding, only then will I do whatever I want. Nothing wrong with going to bed with my own husband. My tongue doesn't hang out like hers when other men pass by.'

Beji was about to speak, but he was swept away by Kamini's torrent of words, and he could no longer remember what he meant to say. Kamini continued, 'You can say the same thing the others do. That I've married many times. Bhorot knows the shastro. He told me there's nothing wrong. Dopdi had five husbands too. The pandobs' mother, she had six children from six husbands.' Having brought a bewildered Beji to the edge of the ravine, she prepared to push him into it. 'Let me tell you something important.'

Important. Again. 'All right,' said a subdued Beji.

'Go spend some time with Bhorot, listen to what he says. You'll see how much he knows. He says a woman is like a river. So many boatmen, so many boats in it. When they pass, there are waves. And a little later, it's back to normal. No sign of their passing.'

Now Beji remembered what he had wanted to say. He interrupted Kamini. 'Stop. Let me finish. Or I'll forget again. I was saying, suppose you were Polashi. And I asked you to marry me. What would you do?'

'What do you mean, what would I do?'

'Would you say yes or no?'

Kamini waved her fist. 'How can I tell you now? I'll think about what to say if you actually ask me. Where the heart is concerned, you never know how it feels. Remember Aurobindo jumping in front of a train? People saved him. He doesn't talk about dying anymore. What I think today is not what I might think tomorrow. And what I thought yesterday ...'

Beji drew a deep breath, filling his lungs with the cloudy sky. Then he said, his voice rising above the rustling leaves, the lapping water and the thump-thump of clothes being washed, 'Then what I'm telling you now is, I want to marry you. What's your answer?'

Kamini's eyes flashed. 'I'm Kamini, not Polashi.'

'I'm talking to Kamini. Will you marry me?'

'What about the rock? The one with Polashi's name carved on it?'

Beji could have given a clever answer. But he made emotion his weapon instead. Summoning tears to his eyes, he said, 'Don't avoid the question. Just tell me, yes or no.'

'What if I say yes? Yes, I'll marry you. Now what?'

'Then come with me.'

'Where?'

'To get married.' Beji took her hand. 'Come.'

'Right now?'

'Yes, now. If we have to do it.'

It had taken Moharaj just a few moments to take his decision. How long could Kamini take for hers? Getting to her feet, she said, 'All right, take me wherever you want to.' Then she laughed, her teeth gleaming like pearls.

'Should I take a bath?' Beji was covered in grime from his scavenging. He wanted to cleanse himself first.

Kamini said, 'Take a dip in the Ganga at Kalighat before you put the sidoor on me. I'll take a dip too. We'll start a new life.'

She quickly took off the sari she was wearing, and put on a freshly washed one.

9

Imaan. The word means honesty, trustworthiness. It was a name, too, of a young man nearing twenty, who was innocent about the world. A newcomer to this locality. Normally, it was impossible to wander in from another area and find a place to stay, unless someone influential offered help. But it proved easy for Imaan, thanks to Roton Mukherjee. A certificate from a good man usually meant exaggerations, but when a known bad character was generous in his praise, he couldn't be disbelieved.

Of course, it was unfair to call Roton a bad character. He wasn't embarrassed about his profession. If asked about it, he said, 'It says in the bus, you are responsible for your possessions. If you can't keep them safe, it's your problem, not someone else's.'

Once, One-Armed Paanu's father was on his way to Kolay Market in Sealdah to buy vegetables cheaply. He wanted to feed the poor on his spiritual guru's birthday. The money was in the pocket of his panjaabi, which was where it was stolen from.

It wasn't a lot of money, but Paanu's father was deeply hurt. He saved five to ten rupees every day of the year precisely for this purpose. It wasn't so much the amount as an audit of his good deeds and bad.

Paanu had been in jail a long time, while Roton was a regular visitor, which was why they knew each other. They were familiar to each other earlier too, by virtue of operating in the same area, but that was different. Each considered the other a 'taabu'—a member of the babu class—and therefore dishonest, scheming and evil. But once they had met in jail, they learnt the truth—they were fellow-travellers, and decent people, both.

So the relationship had continued even after they were released. That was when Paanu confided in Roton. 'He's growing old, my father, who knows when he might die. He has one last wish, to use the money he's saved to feed the poor. But it's been stolen. Twelve hundred, straight from his pocket. I can't manage so much, my trader hasn't paid me yet. I barely managed to pay them off at the police station. I'm broke now, I don't know what to do. Can you do something? I'll pay you back in a week or two.'

Roton said in surprise, 'Oh, that was your father? Oh fuck, it was I who did it. How would I know, I've never met him. First deal of the day, couldn't let go. The train wasn't too crowded, it was a bit of a risk. I wouldn't have given it back if it had been anyone else. But what to do, here you are. I might as well do something for the poor too.'

With a chuckle, Roton continued, 'Your father's my father, my father's yours. Your mother's my mother, my mother's yours. Yes or no? Your wife's my wife ...'

Paanu waited for what should have followed, but Roton paused.

'Say it,' Paanu said.

'Say what?'

'My wife's your wife.'

'I did already—your wife's my wife.'

'And *your* wife?'

'My wife's *my* wife.' Roton smiled mischievously.

Pretending to be angry, Paanu said, 'Want to be beaten up, you fucker?'

'*Maarbo ekhane laash porbe shawshane*?'

'No, you fucker, not the crematorium, your body will end up somewhere that you can't even tell your parents about. Enough with the jokes, hand it over.'

After he'd got the money back, Paanu said, 'You've been a great help, Roton, I'll never forget.'

It was this mutual trust that made Roton take Imaan to Paanu. 'You've seen him before,' he said, 'he was in Central. Entered in his mother's arms, walked out on his own feet. Many years passed in between. Who do I entrust him to? I don't want Imaan to take up my kind of work. So I've brought him to you, give him something to do.'

'Can he read and write?'

'No.'

'Didn't he learn in jail?'

'You know what that's like. Your name, your father's name, that's about all. Why do you want someone with an education?'

'Could have kept my books. What work do I give him?'

'Give him a sack, let him go on rounds.'

'Tell me, Roton, do you really want to make this Glaxo baby do menial labour? His beautiful fair skin will look like coal after an hour in the sun. Is he up to it?'

Roton said, 'Let him do it for some time, let him get hardened to these things. Once he's learnt his way around, I'll find another line of work for him. He'll be set for life if I can get him a job at one of those automobile garages in Garia. Two years there and he can start his own garage.'

Paanu couldn't say no anymore. He took on Imaan as a ragpicker. In any case, the Nandibagan area had no one at the moment; rodbaaj Gopal hadn't dared go back. There was plenty of scrap on the roads there, all of it was going waste. Gopal was worried that the boys' club members of Nandibagan would skin him alive if they caught him. Whether anyone else recognised him or not, the man who ran the tea-stall where he drank tea every day certainly would. He could point Gopal out to the club members. Gopal had stolen plenty of things from the houses around the area. Meanwhile, the torn slippers, plastic and lots of other valuable scrap was rotting. Paanu had been worried about that, so it was an easy choice for him.

'Go north from Palpara,' he instructed Imaan. 'Beyond Rambabur Baajar lies Nandibagan, followed by Kayosthopara. That's the end of your territory. Don't take the road on the left, it belongs to the Kasba party. If you take their stuff away, they'll give you a thrashing. Don't go beyond Kayosthopara. If the sack feels too heavy, get one of those rickshaw trailers. Start tomorrow.'

Paanu's scrap godown was quite large. A long structure adjacent to the railway line, with walls of bamboo tatty and tin, and tiled roof. It could hold six or seven truckful of material. Newspapers, magazines, bottles and other valuable stuff were stored here. Everything else scavenged from the roads lay outside. Any delay in transferring material from the godown to the trucks meant little hillocks springing up. And things happened behind those mounds in the afternoons, with the young men and women taking part in equal measure and with matching enthusiasm.

Paanu knew all about the young women who sold scrap to him. He was given to addressing them with the names of film heroines. Gathering them around him, he said, 'Listen all you Sridevis and Hema Malinis, you're aware I know everything each of you is up to, don't you? This boy, his name is Imaan, don't try to spoil him. He knows nothing of this world, don't ruin his life, any of you. Syphilis, AIDS ... I have no idea what diseases you have. Make sure he doesn't get them. Stay away. If I find out you've disobeyed me'—Paanu pointed to his amputated arm—'this is what lies in wait for you.'

While the women grumbled amongst themselves, Paanu turned his attention to Imaan. He had to be warned too. 'Look my boy,' he said, 'it's a jungle out there. Tigers and hyenas everywhere. All the people you see around you are prowling for human flesh—one chance and they'll pounce on you. Oh ... you don't even know what a jungle is.'

After some thought, Paanu continued, 'All right, think of the world as a gigantic prison. And everyone around you is a murderer or criminal or hangman. Just like in the jail you were in. You know the difference though? In the jail, everyone's details are known. They have a case history which is written up. But not here. By the time we find out, it's too late. There was a gentleman, a retired college professor, with a beautiful two-storeyed house, right here in the neighbourhood. His wife was dead, and both their daughters were married. He lived alone and a maid came in to cook for him. And there was a young girl whom the old man paid to live in the house and look after him. A very courteous, friendly man. Except one day we found out he used to rape the little girl, a poor helpless village girl younger than his grandchildren, day in and day out. The girl had finally reported everything to the cook. That was when the professor's real nature was revealed. But the damage was done. So, you must be very careful. Looks, clothes, a nice house and car, constant use of English, even the attire of a holy man, or a leader who weeps his heart out at public meetings—don't trust any of it. Don't listen to what people are saying. Keep your eyes open for what they're doing. This might help you identify a person's real character. Don't be upset if you discover a political do-gooder has actually sold off truckloads of food grains meant for cyclone victims, or despatches cows to be sold to Bangladesh. The things that happen here do not happen in jail. This is my own learning that I'm passing on to you. It'll help you if you remember them.'

An emaciated young woman was perched on her stuffed sack, picking lice out of her hair and killing them noisily one by one with her nails, savouring the sound of their dying. Glancing at her, Paanu said, 'Why don't you tell us what your own father's been doing with you, Katrina Kaif.'

'Fuck off,' she snarled. 'What's done is done. What's the use of squeezing old stories for new people. Fate. Happened.'

She walked off in a huff, unwilling to have her life turned into a subject of entertainment.

Paanu turned back to Imaan. 'You have no idea what beasts are on the prowl here. But you'll find out slowly. Do you know why I'm throwing you among them? I could have protected you instead. But that will only harm you; you won't learn anything about the world. You must learn to stand on your own two feet. Living at the mercy of others or as their dependents is no way to live. Going around with that sack on your shoulder, you'll see a thousand people, you'll hear a thousand things, and you'll become self-reliant. You won't have to depend on anyone's kindness. And once you know what's what, you can decide for yourself whether to be the hunter or the prey.'

Paanu was in an excellent mood today, dispensing wisdom with great generosity. Calling out to a boy who was passing by, he said, 'You, Shah Rukh, take the mug and bring ten rupees worth of black tea. Four cups.'

'Ten bucks not enough for four cups,' the boy said.

'Who says? Tell him it's me. And get two rupees worth of bidis too.'

Paanu turned back to the women. 'What was I telling you?'

A saucy young woman said, 'Can't speak for the others, but I don't have any diseases. You can check for yourself, or send that Glaxo baby of yours. You can blame me afterwards if you find something wrong.'

'It'll be too late then. No medicine for AIDS. Death is assured. I've been watching all of you ever since Imaan got here. Don't any of you dare try hanky-panky with him. If you do ...'

'Yes, you've told us what you'll do. Say something else,' the young woman said.

Polashi wasn't happy with the way Paanu kept looking at her. There were so many others here, but his glance turned extra meaningful only for her. Fuck it, who was a saint around here? But just look at them feigning innocence. Not that Polashi couldn't turn into a hermit if she wanted to. All she needed was to make up her mind.

Take Aayna from Nayabad, the one who ran the bhaater hotel in front of the minibus-stop, what about her? She was a hermit now, with a shrine inside her home and her hair all matted. She didn't even glance at men anymore. When she met anyone from her past, she said, 'That woman is dead, I'm someone else.'

What about the fifteen intervening years, though? As she said herself, 'I never counted, must have been a thousand or more.' She also said, 'There'll be earthquakes if I so much as even mention whose moles I've seen and where. I've had countless hotshots naked in my bed. I ate off a new plate every day, never re-used an old one.'

Aayna was much older than Polashi, but somehow the two of them had developed an intimacy. Whenever she went in that direction on her rounds, Polashi spent some time at Aayna's hotel and got herself a drink of water. Aayna cooked in a coal-fired earthen stove set on the pavement, and stored the rice and curry in a pot inside a small kiosk. A table and a bench in front of it had room for three, four at a squeeze. All the minibus drivers and conductors, as well as porters, labourers and rickshaw-drivers with low earnings, ate here. Aayna cooked very well, and used tasty spices, which meant a long queue every afternoon, with one customer being speedily replaced by another.

Polashi was certainly surprised at the way Aayna had spent her days before her transformation, for she used to live in an area where the licentious ways of the rail bosti were not the norm.

They had been talking one day when there was a bus strike, so that there were very few customers.

'Doesn't anyone say anything to you?' Polashi had asked.

'Who will say anything?

'Neighbours?'

'Do any of them pay for my upkeep? I don't even live in a rented house. This place is mine. Which bastard can say anything to me here? I can dance naked in my own house if I like, no fucker or his father can object. I don't go peeping into their houses, why should they decide what I can or cannot do in mine? Not that I do anything in anyone's face. I believe in decency. I respect everyone. If someone's visiting and someone else wants to know who it is, I say it's a relative from Behala or Baruipur. Any relation will do, who's checking? It isn't as though they don't know, but they don't say anything because everyone knows I can let the cat out of the bag about all of them.'

Aayna laughed. 'A doddering old fellow came one day. Not a tooth in his mouth. Lives up Hazra Road. Someone asked, who's the old coot? I said, my father.'

Polashi objected. 'Old men. You like it with them?'

Aayna said casually, 'No man ever gets old. Who cares if the axe is ancient. All you need to check is if it's sharp enough.'

'That's all very well,' Polashi said, 'but how can you do it with someone you've just said is your father.'

'Father or fucker, who knows,' Aayna said contemptuously. 'There's no need to be blatant about it. They want it kept under wraps, so I do it.'

After a pause she continued, 'Some people have bought land here and built houses. They're always talking of right and wrong. I know these pricks inside out. So one day they came to my shop and said, you can't go on this way. No more of getting men from other places into your house every night. Our children must not see all this. So I lost my temper and said, I'm not married. It's an old habit, can't sleep at night without a man. Now you're saying, I can't bring in outsiders. All right then, I won't. You people can make a timetable to decide who will be with me on different nights. Binoy Biswas had just become the secretary of the association. He's the one with the tea-stall near the bus-stop. He has a wart near his groin. Like they say, the thief has the loudest voice, so he shouts at me, what do you think you're saying, Aayna. How dare you say such a thing to us? That was it. I said, fix yourself before fixing the neighbourhood, Biswas dada, don't you shout before that! Remember you were in my house one rainy day? And your son came in with an umbrella at the same time? You hid beneath my bed. And today you dare scream at me? That shut him up good and proper.'

Aayna laughed and then continued, 'One more thing, Poli, and it's not just me, Taslima on East Road will say the same thing. She's educated, comes from a good family, works as an ayah at a nursing home. She says it too. There's no other relationship between men and women besides the one between the legs. Call them anything, kaka or mama or baap—a woman shouldn't trust any man. So many fathers have knocked up their own daughters. It's come out in the papers too. I won't tell you their names. They're well-known leaders now, respected by society. Obviously they don't recognise me anymore. But before they got so important, they would be rolling in the dust on the floor of my house. That Shundor babu—he's a councillor now—he even got me pregnant. He had to take me to Basanti to clear it out. He would have been in serious trouble had anyone found out. But I won't lie—that would be wrong—Shundor Chowdhury paid for some of the land I bought to build my house. He got me my ration card and voter card too.'

Aayna had poured out the story of her life that day. 'You know Kumirmari on the Sundarban side? That's where I used to live. We're from Bangladesh. We came over the year there was a big war and started living in Kumirmari. My father had died already. It was just my mother, my two brothers, and me. Those two got married and moved out—they didn't take care of ma and me. How could they—they earned very little as daily labourers, they could barely support themselves. So Ma sent me off to Calcutta with someone. I was maybe fifteen or sixteen. This person put me to work with a family. It was a four-storeyed building, each floor occupied by one of four brothers. Common kitchen. I got food, clothes and fifty rupees a month. Nothing much to say about the work, it's the same everywhere. But the eldest of the four brothers was a perfect chodkhor. Divorced, drank all day, did no work. Spent all his time in his room, and dragged me off whenever he could. To the attic, beneath the stairs, the bathroom, his own bedroom. But I won't lie, I didn't mind it. It was new. I quite enjoyed it in fact. And he'd give me some money every time not to tell anyone. I'd saved around eleven or twelve hundred this way. One day, his sister-in-law caught us, and sacked me immediately. I found work elsewhere, but it was the same story. The first man was young, but this one was halfway to death. But yes, he did give me a hundred or two hundred each time. I was young, too frightened and embarrassed to say anything or tell anyone. One day, his daughter found out what he was up to, so I lost my job again. Wherever I went to work, it was my body they reached out for. I realised my body held value even if I didn't. Everyone paid, and I managed to save about four thousand. Sometime later, when I was working at a house in Jadavpur, I began to wonder how long I could go on this way. I was older now, and learning to think for myself. One day, I heard there was land going cheap at Nayabad. Farmers were selling the land that had been seized from jomidaars and handed over to them. Poor people were buying it and building houses. Gojen, a rickshaw-driver I knew, took me along to make enquiries. I used my savings to buy a bit of land here and make a house with tatty walls and a tiled roof. Shundor Chowdhury added to the land sometime later. I brought my mother to live with me, but she died three years later. Sometime after moving here, I had a relationship with this boy. It began with his visits to sleep with me, but soon I found I had fallen in love with him. He knew how to talk sweet—you have beautiful hair, you have lovely eyes, I love you so much, I can't live without you. I was carried away. I would be miserable if he skipped a day. Then, he stopped coming altogether, and I found out he had got married. I felt like I'd been plunged into darkness. Living without him seemed pointless. I had five litres of kerosene at home. I poured it on myself and lit a match. Someone was passing by, he collected a group of people and they took me to hospital. I had seventy per cent burns, but still I didn't die. I came home alive after three and a half months. But the woman who returned was completely different from the woman who went to hospital. There in my hospital bed I had decided that I had died, and this was a new life. I wouldn't let men toy with me anymore, they would become my playthings. They wouldn't lie on my breast anymore—I'd dance on theirs.'

Aayna paused for breath. 'It became an addiction. I couldn't sleep without a man in my bed. But I had no one paarment; no one stayed. Even earlier they wouldn't, and now with scars everywhere on my body except my face, there was no question. So I let in anyone who wanted to spend the night, but I never allowed them more than once or at most two times. I was frightened. Men are swines, they will say the sweetest things to sleep with you. What if I ended up believing some son of a bitch and fell in love with him? Then I'd want to set myself on fire again. So if anyone came back a third time, I threw them out with insults. This one time I made one of them sleep in the veranda while taking another man into my room. He left in the morning, never came back. Men are bastards. They will fuck a dozen women—no harm in that—but they will be hurt if they see someone they've slept with allowing another man into her bed. But I make it very clear to them. Stay tonight if you like, my room may not be available tomorrow. Every night is my wedding night. Which is how the number may be a thousand or more—I haven't kept track.'

This was the same Aayna, who would say she couldn't sleep without a man in her bed. She had forsaken that existence entirely to become a hermit. She still ran her hotel, and her customers were unchanged. But if anyone knocked on her door at night like in the old days, she charged at them with a boti. 'Go to the women in your own home, you bastard, what do you want with me?'

Polashi knew she could follow in Aayna's footsteps if she wanted to; she could say, 'Enough, no more.' But no one would allow her to fast. Someone would turn up at her doorstep, throw themselves at her feet and weep, or, if she brandished a boti, demand to be killed by her. She felt pity when they behaved this way.

Take Chhotka, the renowned neighbourhood goon. A few months ago, he had chopped up a young man named Kolyan, a competitor of his in the moneylending business. He went to jail for it, and was now out on bail from the High Court. There was no counting the number of others he had killed. That time in Bhringigram, when there was violence for two or three months over ownership of land, Chhotka and his gang were hired by the party in power. When he came back, Chhotka himself had confessed to Polashi one night, 'There was no time to count. Kill, stuff in a sack, throw into the river. I'm telling you, don't you tell anyone else.' But even the fearsome murderer turned into a pleading beggar at her door.

One day, Polashi had asked him, 'I heard hundreds of girls were raped in Bhringigram. How many did you rape?'

'Not one,' declared Chhotka. 'I saw others do it, but not me. I don't get anything out of forcing anyone. When a woman is frightened, she withdraws into her shell. Yes or no?'

'How would I know? No one's ever tried to force me.'

'You'll know if they do. That's no fun. You fuck for pleasure. You can't get that pleasure from rape or even from paying a whore. You may not even get it from your wife—our girls are too shy. But I don't need to tell you any of this—you're an artist, you know the art of driving a man mad. That's why I keep coming back to you.'

Imaan was a child for all intents and purposes. He may have grown physically, but mentally he was immature and underdeveloped. He had been released from jail, but in his head, he was still imprisoned within the four walls of prison. Polashi felt the urge to break those walls and give him the true taste of freedom, so he would become a real man. This was why she had been staring at him covetously. Paanu had noticed. And though he hadn't named anyone, Polashi felt he was referring to her in particular. This was bothering her now.

10

'What kind of education did you get, Paanu-da?' Imaan had asked.

'Why do you want to know, Imaan?'

'The way you talk is so similar to the way all those learned men in jail used to talk.'

'No, I never really studied properly. I can sign my name, that's about all.'

'How come you talk like schoolteachers then? Barin Sen in jail used to say the same things.'

'Did you learn anything from Barin babu?'

'No.'

'I was in jail too. I heard Barin babu and others like him. I memorised some of the things they told me. Those are the things I pass on to all of you from time to time, in case it proves useful.'

Today, Imaan was feeling unusually philosophical as he stood by Moharaj's corpse. What was life? Nothing at all. A hot glass of tea in someone's hand, which could fall to the ground and be shattered if a pebble was thrown at it.

Moharaj was alive a short while ago, and now he wasn't. Even if he hadn't jumped into the path of a train, he could still have faced a similar death. A train could have hit him anyway. Considering the speed with which it passed, it could be derailed easily and hit Moharaj's shack.

Imaan had never seen a train in his life before coming to Jadavpur. He had not yet taken a ride in one. Where would he go? He hadn't wanted to either; he was afraid. What if he slipped?

Now he mused. Just as the person standing here is me, the one lying there is me too. This small difference between standing and lying down, the little time that it took for the change, is all there is by way of life. I don't know how much time I have, no one does. The line from one point to the other would be a long one for some, short for others. Some would make the journey at the speed of a snail, others like a fast car.

As these thoughts raced through his mind, Imaan heard a voice in his head say, 'I'm alive as long as I'm on my feet. I'm still standing, I haven't lain myself down yet. We'll see about that when the time comes, but I must do something important before that.' He had to start now, here, where he was.

People were saying that Moharaj's death was not so much suicide as it was murder. And the person they were holding responsible was Shaadhin Shorongi. They were blaming Ranibala too, but the primary role was Shaadhin babu's. Still, would it do any good now to beat him up mercilessly?

'Move aside, make way.'

Two people pushed through the crowd with a long bamboo pole and a large gunny sheet. Placing Moharaj's severed corpse on it, they trussed it up with a rope. Experienced hands. The body was tied to the pole. One of them took photographs, and another entered some details in a register. 'So hot,' the writer said. 'So much fucking rain but still doesn't get cooler. Who's here from the dead body's family? Come to the office. I'll finish the paperwork there.'

Ranibala was crying loudly at this time for obvious reasons. Ram and Baloram were crying along with her. She had been cooking and had forgotten to take the pan off the stove. The smell of charred food spread through the air.

Imaan turned his head at the soft sound near his shoulder to find Polashi standing behind him, her body in contact with his. For some reason, his heart began to hammer, he felt an electric current running down his spine. Polashi had a reckless air, as though she had killed someone or was about to kill someone. They had met almost every day these past two months, coming close to each other but never speaking. Imaan felt his tongue was dry from fear at the quietly cruel look in Polashi's eyes, like a gun with a silencer. What was she trying to say?

Polashi had asked herself many times why she couldn't turn her eyes away from Imaan. What do you look for in that fool? What does he have that no one else has? There's something, her eyes replied, I can't express it, but I want to keep looking.

Polashi was constantly surprised by Imaan. How could a grown-up man be so naive? Men of his age in the rail bosti fathered two or three children by this time. Some of them even left one woman for another. This one was a child. Polashi felt the urge to mould him in her own way, make him hers.

She couldn't tell anyone of this secret wish of hers. Kamini could guess some of it, but Polashi wasn't ready to confess to her. What if the same desire was burning within Kamini too? She would become a competitor then.

Still, Polashi had to bare her heart to someone. She had to find a way out of this fire. Else there was no peace by day, no sleep at night. Living would become difficult at this rate. There was only one person she could talk to about all this. Aayna. So she went off to meet her one afternoon.

'Long time. You don't come by these days,' said Aayna.

'Not enough scraps here. Not worth the trouble.'

'What brings you here today?'

'To ask you for advice.'

'Go on.'

After the preliminaries, Polashi got to the point. 'There's a new boy at the station. Much younger. But my body feels funny every time I see him—I go mad. I can't control myself, I feel like jumping on him.'

'Very handsome?'

'There's no one like him over there.'

'Yes, you get these people. They don't even have to be handsome. But there's something irresistible about them.'

'My heart jumps when I see him, I don't know what to do. I don't feel like working or eating or talking to anyone or anything at all. Tell me the way out.'

'It's not just you,' said Aayna, 'many people have such feelings. Some for someone of the same age, some for someone much younger, some for much older. Just the other day, a woman of sixty in Punjab married a boy of twenty-six. It was on TV. And then old men of seventy marry girls their granddaughters' age. Why? That's the kind of companion they desire.'

'That's what's happened to me.'

'I see nothing wrong with it. No one would think it strange even if you married someone your father's age. But they'll say things if you marry someone ten years younger. They'll say it behind your back, if not in front of you. But the heart—how do you control it?'

After some thought, Aayna continued, 'Haven't you heard about men being caught sleeping with young girls? And when they get desperate, they rape the girl. They know it's wrong, they know they can go to jail if caught, but still they do it—they lose their heads. But only men can do that. Women can't rape. So you have to win his heart.'

'How? He doesn't even lift his eyes, leave alone talk to me.'

'Oh, he will. If not today, then tomorrow. Stick to him like a shadow, give him a feel of your body now and then. Fan his hidden desire. You have no idea the things I did with my half-burnt body. And look at you, you're flawless. Be patient, and things will go your way.'

Some twenty fishermen and their families lived in small shacks on state-owned land on the bank of the Sarbamangala river. Polashi had spent her childhood and adolescence in one of those shacks. Her father used to go looking for fish in canals and ponds and lakes, and her mother used to tend to hens and ducks and do the housework. Their days were marked by scarcity, and they often had to starve. Still, that was something Polashi could endure. What she couldn't endure was the way her father tormented them, beating up both Polashi and her mother. She herself was naughty sometimes, which might have angered him, but she didn't know why he beat her mother, who was always soft-spoken. There was nowhere to run away to, so they had to tolerate his behaviour.

It wasn't just him, of course. All the men there were the same. All of them beat up their wives on the slightest pretext, the way thieves were beaten up on being caught. In fact, even thieves got more mercy compared to wives. If a man's wife died, he could get another one. And with society sanctioning the dowry system, this meant there was a chance of economic gain too. This was why the men seemed to beat their wives with the intention of killing them, but somehow or the other they survived. No one stopped their neighbours. 'It's their affair, what can we say?'

This was how Polashi's mother died one day. Witnessing such inhuman torture from her childhood had disposed Polashi towards hating men. A mixture of fear and rage had robbed her of all trust in men, a race with whose members she couldn't possibly live together. They would make her life hell if she depended on one of them. So Polashi had vowed never to marry.

But this was no modern city; girls here had no independence. When Polashi turned fourteen, her father began to make arrangements to get her married. By then, he had got married again, and her stepmother was even more violent with her than her father. So Polashi left home one day. But she had already had some sexual experience before that.

That was a year earlier. She had gone swimming in the river, assuring herself that there was no one nearby. What she didn't know was that someone had been watching her, not just that day, but earlier too, and was lying in wait. His name was Shyamacharon. He lived nearby, and Polashi addressed him as mama, since he was her stepmother's brother. When she got out of the water, Shyamacharon grabbed her before she could get dressed, drawing her deep inside the field of jute nearby. Since she knew him, Polashi wasn't frightened, but she was embarrassed because she was naked. And astonished, when he made her lie down on the ground and prepared to lie on top of her. 'What are you doing, mama,' she had said. 'Let me go.'

'Wait,' he said, 'you'll like it.' This man, as old as her father, had mounted her.

Polashi had seen animals do it, and knew humans did it too. She was curious about how it happened, and today her curiosity was met. It didn't feel too bad, in fact; she had mixed feelings afterwards. Shyamacharon had told her not to tell anyone, and even given her two rupees to keep her mouth shut. Polashi didn't tell anyone, using the money to buy two different kinds of sweets the next two days. A few days later, someone drew her into the jute field again. This time it wasn't Shyamacharon but his son Abhoy. These experiences in her adolescence had told Polashi that although men were bad, there was a magic in their bodies that nothing else could provide.

Polashi was not yet fifteen when she ran away from home and took a train to the city. She was sitting on the platform after she got off the train, not knowing where to go. That was when she met Pawddo-r ma, her aunt. When Polashi's aunt found out why she was here, she said, 'What have you done! With those looks you won't be safe here at all. What will you do if someone lures you to a brothel and sells you there? There's no escape once you're stuck in a third-floor room.'

Seeing Polashi brought back all her grief for Pawddo, her lost daughter. 'I had a daughter like you. That son of a whore Nitai took her away somewhere. I haven't heard from her in four years. The swine came here with the handpump mechanic. We never found out who the fuck he was or where he had come from. My idiot girl ran away him. Someone told me she was in Sonagachhi, so I found out the address and went there, but the doorman refused to let me in.'

It was Pawddo-r ma who got Polashi employed by a family where she worked as a cook herself. They had been looking for a full-time maid.

Here at the age of seventeen, Polashi experienced the male touch on her pleasure spots again. The man who drove the family car invited her for sex inside the vehicle, to which she agreed at once.

Pawddo-r ma, who had not been keeping well, left the job after some time. And soon afterwards, the head of the family caught Polashi and the driver in the act. He had no moral objection since both of them were beneath his social class, but he was furious because they were doing it on his expensively upholstered car seats. He slapped the driver several times, and because he couldn't do the same thing to a girl, he sacked Polashi at once.

So Polashi moved in with Pawddo-r ma who lived near the station. She used the money she had saved so far to build a bamboo tatty shack by the railway line. Then, just like Bindu, Kushum or Oholya, she hoisted her sari above her knees, tied a gamchha around her waist, and set off on her rounds as a ragpicker. Don't give a fuck for anyone—live as you please, do what you want.

One-Armed Paanu was stunned into silence the first time that Polashi had shown up to ask for a sack. Did she seriously mean to move about the streets on her own? What if some mad dog jumped on her? A worried Paanu did what he had done for no other woman. He had bought her a packet of chilli powder. 'Keep this with you at all times. Throw it in the eyes of anyone who tries to act nasty.'

The opportunity to use it had never arisen. She lived in the shack she had made herself. A free life without any constraints. She remembered what Aayna had said: every night a wedding night, with a new groom.

The currents on which she had floated had now brought Polashi near two young men. Beji and Imaan. Both younger than her. One of them was mad about her; one she was mad about. One of them couldn't look away from her; the other one never even looked at her.

But it was One-Armed Paanu's warning to stay away from Imaan that got her back up. All right then, let's see if you can protect him.

Going up to Imaan, Polashi smiled alluringly. 'How much today? Two hundred?'

'No,' said Imaan. 'One eighty.'

'Why're you behaving like a new bride? Do you think I'm a tiger about to eat you up? Look at me. What happened yesterday? I heard you got beaten up.'

'No, they couldn't catch me. I ran as soon as I heard them.'

'It keeps happening.' Polashi rolled her eyes. 'If you sleep on the platform, you have to take all this. The days the GRP or RPF come on their rounds, they don't stop to see who they're beating up. Sitaram was sleeping on his back. They kicked him so hard in his ribs, he had to go straight to hospital.'

'But, didi, we ...'

'Don't you call me didi! I'm not your sister, elder or younger. Call me by my name.'

'All right. What I was saying was, we were only sleeping after a hard day's work, we weren't harming anyone. Why did the police start beating us up? They don't even beat anyone in jail that way for nothing.'

'It's not for nothing. Nobody beats anyone up for nothing. They did it to clear out the platform. There are always women in the station who've missed the last train, maids or vegetable-sellers, maybe. The police were going to fuck them, and you'd be witnesses if you remained. So they beat up one or two, and the rest ran away. Last night, they raped two women. They were crying near the signal. No use crying, what's done is done.'

Imaan said, 'This is wrong. They're supposed to protect everyone.'

'Don't talk of right and wrong here. What are you and I going to be able to do about it? What I say is, don't sleep in the station anymore. You could be the next one with a boot in your ribs.'

'Where should I sleep then? Is any place safe here? Someone was sleeping on the pavement. I heard he was run over by a car.'

'Yes, pavements are dangerous that way. Drivers are often drunk at night. Why don't you sleep in Paanu-da's godown?'

'I tried. So hot, so many mosquitoes too. Couldn't sleep a wink.'

'What to do then,' Polashi said after some thought. 'Stay on the platform, hope for the best.' She wanted to say more, but the words stuck in her throat.

'I've heard rooms are available on rent here,' said Imaan. 'With a fan and a light and everything.'

'They are, but you can't afford them. Have you any idea of the rent? Paying for a month will clean you out. There are also rooms where the babus live, but they won't give those to a ragpicker chhotolok like you or me. A maid had used her entire life's savings to buy a feylat in Garfa. The babus didn't let her enter.'

'Why didn't they let her enter?'

'She used to work in their houses elsewhere before they bought a feylat in that building. Now how could they let her stay as their equal? Babus would lose their prestige. Same with you. If they let you rent a room, what will happen to their prestige?'

'Then I won't get a room.'

'Unless you can wear decent clothes and look in an area where they don't know you. But even if they say yes, they'll want to know who's in your feymilee. Do you have a feymilee?'

'What's a feymilee?'

'Wife. Children. Do you have any?' Polashi smiled mischievously. 'Tell me, do you?'

'No.'

'Not even half or quarter?'

'Everyone here would have known if I did.'

'We'd have known if it was full feymilee. No one talks about half or quarter.'

'I don't have any.'

'Then get married quickly. Easy to get a room after that.'

Imaan couldn't see the connection. Polashi explained, 'Everyone has a feymilee of their own. Letting an unmarried young man into the house is asking for trouble. What if you do something with their daughter or wife or someone? There'll be a scandal. If you're married, your wife will keep you in check. If she sees things getting out of hand, she'll scream or cry, and make trouble for you. And the landlord will throw you out. But it's really difficult to live in the station nowadays. If it's not the police, it's goons or drunkards. The GRP has a quota it seems. They have to arrest a certain number every month, or no promotion. So they just pick people up and slap charges on them. Then these people rot for ninety days in jail for no crime.'

Imaan wasn't worried about ninety days in jail, but he was afraid of being beaten up. But then, he was even more afraid of getting married. Jonardon, the rickshaw-driver, had warned him that it was like being a lifer in prison. So he said firmly, 'I'm not getting married.'

Polashi was surprised at the determination in his voice. 'Why? You don't like girls?'

Imaan shook his head.

Polashi spoke through clenched teeth. 'I've heard one man becomes another's wife in jail. Nowadays it's happening outside too. To each his own. So were you someone's wife in jail? And now you can't give up old habits to become someone's husband instead?'

Imaan turned red. 'What are you saying? I don't do such things.'

'Then why don't you like girls?'

'Of course, I like girls. When did I say I didn't? Everyone likes girls.'

'Never mind everyone, do you?'

'I told you I do.'

'Do you like me? I'm a girl.'

'A lot,' Imaan mumbled.

'Thank heavens. I thought ... never mind.' Polashi laughed in relief. She felt as moved by his confession as by a man's arms around her. The door seemed to be opening. Maybe she would be able to enter one day. But she had to be patient.

The doms had left with Moharaj's body. With nothing left to gape at, the crowd was dispersing. Polashi remembered it had been a while since Kamini had left with Beji to bathe. Oh well, win some lose some. Let Beji go. Let Kamini go too. She could live alone with her dream.

It was time she had a bath too, it was getting on for evening. 'Have you had a bath?' she asked Imaan. 'Let's go to the pond.' She led him by the hand, and he followed her obediently. After a pause, Polashi said, 'Jongol-da is dead, but he's moving about the bosti as a spirit. Moharaj-da died of an accident. He has no choice but to become a ghost. My house is on the edge of the pond, lots of trees all around it. I feel scared there all the time. I have no idea how I'll live there now.'

Polashi was expecting a response, but Imaan didn't oblige. He didn't know what to say. His expression didn't reveal whether he believed in ghosts or not.

Polashi continued, 'I have such a big room—too big for someone living alone. I'm thinking of putting up a curtain down the middle and giving out half the room. Whether I get rent or not, having someone nearby will make me feel better, don't you think?'

'Of course,' said Imaan. 'It's so helpful to have someone nearby in times of trouble.'

You're afraid of the police and goons and drunkards, Imaan, I'm afraid of ghosts. You can be my courage, I can be your sanctuary. Say it, you wretch, can I rent your room, Polashi?

The ardent plea remained unsaid at first, but eventually, the heart won the battle with the brain. 'Want to stay in my room? We're out all day, it's just a matter of sleeping at night. Want to? I have two mosquito nets, I'll give you one. The window faces south, the breeze is better than any electric fan. I'll feel safe if you're there. Will you stay with me, Imaan?'

Imaan remembered Paanu's warning. It wouldn't be right to do anything without asking him. So he said, 'Let me think it over.' Then he plunged into the water.

'Do you know how to swim, Imaan?'

'I'm staying near the edge in shallow water.'

'What good is that? The real fun is in the middle of the pond. Want to learn swimming? I can teach you. I'm a village girl. All of us there knew how to swim. We've swum across lakes so many times.'

In her head, Polashi added, 'I can teach you how to swim, I can teach you how to drown too. If I can take you into the middle, you can't depend on anyone but me. Want to learn how to swim, Imaan?'

11

It was the busy morning hour on the street which wasn't particularly wide. Office-goers were rushing towards buses and trains, children were going to school. Shoppers were on their way to buy fish, meat and vegetables; some were returning on foot and some in rickshaws. Thousands of people pursuing thousands of tasks.

A lorry was standing in the middle of the street. No one would have objected if it had been parked in an orderly manner. But it was standing diagonally, its front stretching to the middle of the road, and its back touching a potato godown. Sacks of potatoes were being unloaded noisily by four porters. They would have had to traverse a longer distance with their sacks had the lorry been parked as it should have. But this had hampered the movement of traffic, and a jam had ensued, even blocking pedestrians.

Vegetable-sellers took up position every day on either side of the godown and on both pavements. They had no shops, this was the only way they could sell their vegetables. But right now, passers-by were screaming and swearing. Komol Shamonto, the owner of the godown, paid no attention, coolly counting the sacks while drinking tea.

Once the truck had left after being unloaded completely, he tossed his empty teacup away and said, as always, 'Really, people have no patience these days. Not at all cooperative. How long did it take? An hour at most? What harm does it do to take a detour instead of screaming at the truck? How will it help? Will I stop the unloading because of you? Never.'

Now that he was feeling lighter after speaking his mind, he picked up a slip of paper and shouted, 'Load eight sacks, Bheem—six shingur and two chondromukhi. The chondromukhis are for Boudi-r hoteyl, two shingurs for Mihir's grocery, three for the hostel for the handicapped, one for Paik. Oho, Naaraan needs supplies, too, I completely forgot. Make it ten shingurs, Bheem. Go to Naraan's after Mihir's delivery. And then to Boudi's on the way back.'

The plump, middle-aged Bheem mumbled, 'I'll take eight, can't do more. I'll deliver Naraan's stuff tomorrow.'

'Tomorrow? What the fuck do you mean? He's out of potatoes, what's he going to sell?'

'Then ask someone else.'

'You're going the same way, can't you go a little farther and make the delivery? You won't get paid if someone else does it. Don't you need the money?'

'Money!' Bheem groaned. 'My life's in danger, what am I going to do with money.'

And then came his mournful dirge. 'No strength in my body anymore. I could haul twenty sacks at a time earlier, you've seen me do it. But you know what happened to me. How am I going to work hard now? The children are young, so there's no one else to earn. If there was someone who could help, I'd just lie down in bed and never get up.'

It was the same litany every day, which everyone laughed at. Some even joked, 'So, Bheem, can you do it anymore? Can you get it up? You're going to lose your wife if you can't.'

Sometimes it was no longer a joke; it turned into quarrels, with much swearing. Bheem would say, 'Send your wife to me if you want to find out whether I can get it up or not.' But now, he didn't snap back; he only listened to the barbs glumly. What was he to do? He had shot himself in the foot; he would have to take whatever people said.

Komol Shamonto was somewhat distracted today. There were occasional spells of rain, but they didn't dispel the humidity. And now, all the complaints. Annoyed, he said, 'What fucking operation is this that's made you so weak. The illness isn't anywhere in your body, it's in your mind. Be strong, everything will be fine. Gone from fucking twenty sacks to fucking eight. Soon it'll be down to four. You'll starve to death.'

Bheem croaked, 'It's all very well for you to say be strong. How am I supposed to be strong? The mind isn't separate from the body. When the body was powerful, so was the mind. Now the body has gone to hell and so has the mind. You don't know about my physical condition. If you'd had the operation, you'd know how it makes your heart thump.'

'Did you say I haven't had the operation? The fuck you know.'

'You've had it? When?'

'You think I'm going to tell everyone like you do when and where I did it? Thousands of people are having it done every day, you're not the only one in the world. It does no harm. A small fucking operation.'

Despite all the logic, Bheem refused to deliver more than eight sacks. He was convinced he was weaker these days. 'Let's say I'm fine when I leave, but what if I collapse when I'm halfway there?'

Swearing at Bheem, Komol Shamonto turned to Shibpodo. 'See if you can find someone else. Have to send it somehow. If you can't find a trailer, get a rickshaw. Naaraan came all the way specially in the morning to tell me. He will raise hell if he doesn't get his stuff.'

After he had found a trailer and loaded the sacks on it, Shibpodo went up to Komol Shamonto. 'So, dada, you've done it too?'

'What the fuck have I done too?'

'I mean you've had it done down there. It didn't hurt?'

'Obviously it did. But like an ant bite.'

'And you're fine?'

'What does it look like?'

'Yes, I can see you're fine. But what Bheem says scares me. If I can't work, I'll starve to death.'

Komol Shamonto surveyed Shibpodo. 'Why do you need it? What the fuck for? You're not married. And if you do end up with someone now and then, there are pills for that.'

Komol Shamonto suspected something from Shibpodo's depressed demeanour. He'd been going about his work morosely for some days now, not even talking to anyone properly. It was obvious that his usual cheerful self had been ground down by anxiety of some kind. And now he was asking about sterilisation. What was going on? All it needed was a little prodding for Shibpodo to blurt out the truth.

'Aamodi boudi's husband is dead, my wife has run away. She has a child and so do I. So nobody wants more children. But boudi won't agree unless I get the operation done. That's why I was asking about it.'

'Get it done,' Komol Shamonto said with a smile.

The day that Shibpodo took his courage in both hands and lay down on a hospital bed was also the one on which Kamini and Beji got married and discovered each other's bodies. Beji felt he had found the elixir of immortality.

But Imaan was simply not able to adjust in the terrifying friendless society of the free world outside jail. The small walled space in which he had spent his past life was one he knew intimately. He was familiar with every brick and stone and tree and person there. It did not take much effort to realise how good or evil a particular individual was. And because it was a small space with a low population, there were very few bad people. But here, this ocean seemed to be teeming with ferocious creatures. And the trouble was that they could not be identified since everyone had a mask on. There was no knowing when any of them would pounce, or why.

Imaan didn't like it here anymore. He felt like returning to his old place of residence. But going back in was even harder than getting out.

He ran into the deputy jailer of Central Jail one day on his ragpicking rounds. The deputy jailer was visiting his daughter and son-in-law, who lived in the beautiful house named Shujon Nibaash near Rambabur Baajar. Imaan spotted him on his morning walk with his son-in-law's father. Going up to him, Imaan said, 'How are you, saar? Are you well? You look thinner.'

'Oh, it's Imaan.'

Normally a man of his stature would not be having a conversation on the street with a former convict. Not that any convict would have come up to him with such warmth. Anyone who'd been to jail tried to keep that part of his life as much of a secret as possible.

Normally, convicts and jail authorities are at loggerheads with one another, but Imaan had been a unique sort of resident, and had no conflict with either the prisoners or the authorities. So he freely approached the deputy jailer, who, for his part, also responded without any awkwardness. 'I'm very well, Imaan, how are you? How's the world outside treating you?'

The deputy jailer's walking companion looked at him in surprise, astonished by the interest demonstrated by a senior government officer in the life and well-being of a ragpicker. But more surprises were awaiting him. For the deputy jailer turned to him and said, 'Imaan's a very good boy. He was in our jail for many years.' A good boy who was in jail? And for many years, which would make him a major criminal. Convicted of robbery or rape or murder. How could he be a good boy? He was having trouble understanding.

'I'm not well, saar. I was far better off in jail,' Imaan responded ruefully to the deputy jailer's question. 'When I was in jail, I used to think the world outside must be beautiful, the people would be wonderful. But I was wrong, saar. It's only been six months and I'm exhausted. Central Jail is a much better place, saar. The people there are nowhere near as bad.'

'What do you mean?' the deputy jailer asked.

Imaan had plucked some new words out of the constant conversations around him. Now he used some of them. 'Saar, we had about four thousand inmates when I was in jail. No more than fifty of them were actually bad people. They were the ones who made trouble. The rest were all decent; they were kind and compassionate. But, saar, there are lakhs of people here outside jail, and the only decent people I've met in all this time are the pickpocket Roton-da and the scrapdealer Paanu-da. The others all seem to be professional murderers like Kaalu Goaala or robbers like Bihari Singh or rapists like Raghob Sen. I'm not used to living among so many bad people, saar, I don't like it here anymore.'

'Where will you go then?' The deputy jailer said in his head. He wasn't surprised. There were lakhs of criminals in this free world, how many of them had actually been put behind bars? Most had slipped through loopholes in the law.

But although he wasn't taken aback, his son-in-law's father certainly was. How could a prison filled with murderers and goons be a better place than the civilised, educated and cultured society of law-abiding citizens? Why was the deputy jailer saying Imaan was a good boy? Didn't this amount to pointing an accusing finger at honest people? He was affronted.

'It's wonderful to meet you, saar,' said Imaan courteously. 'I've been thinking of going to the jail gate to meet you. I even got into a bus. There was a man on the bus who had been in jail on some political case. He knew me, but he didn't know my circumstances. So he told the other passengers I'm a convicted pickpocket, and they slapped me and threw me out of the bus. So I didn't end up going to see you.'

After a pause, he continued, 'Saar, I don't have a poor record in jail. All of you loved me so much. Will you take me back and let me stay?'

'Take you back where? Let you stay where?' The deputy jailer did not understand.

'Where I was before, the Boys' Ward.'

'Are you talking of going back into jail?'

'Yes, saar. Will you let me stay?'

The deputy jailer didn't know whether to be amused or depressed at Imaan's naiveté. Was he mad, why was he voluntarily offering to give up his free life to live as a prisoner?'

Since he knew Imaan well, he was aware this wasn't a joke, that he was speaking from his heart. So he said compassionately, 'That's not possible, Imaan. No one can be allowed to stay in jail that way.'

Imaan said plaintively, 'Jailer babu and you can do anything you want, saar. You are the maalik. I'll go tomorrow if you ask me to. Who will know I'm there among all those thousands of people? So many people live there on your mercy.'

Imaan was dripping with gratitude now. 'Remember Raghuram, saar? He used to live on the pavement, he had TB. He would have died without treatment if he hadn't gone to jail. The police arrested him in a case of theft because they couldn't find the real culprit, and then you chose to let him stay in jail. That's how he survived. I met him recently. He's become an actual thief now.'

With a tone of worry in his voice, the deputy jailer said, 'It's true what you're saying, many innocent people are, in fact, in jail. But there are rules. Just as we can't let someone go on a whim, we can't take in someone on a whim either. It needs a magistrate's order.'

'How do I get one, saar?'

'You can't get one.' The deputy jailer's words were like bullets from a gun. 'Only if the police arrest you for some reason and present you in court, and only if the magistrate finds a reason to keep you in custody will he give the order.'

Before Imaan could respond, the deputy jailer continued, 'Now you're going to ask what you have to do so that the police arrest you and present you in court. The simple answer is that you have to do something that's considered a crime according to the Indian Penal Code. Steal something, rob someone, cheat someone, kill someone. Can you do any of these? I know you very well, you can't. So you can never go to jail.'

So as long as I'm alive, it has to be in this horrifying place among all these horrible people, Imaan thought to himself. It was very difficult to live like this. Suffering this way till one died was worse than death itself. This wasn't how things were in jail. No one persecuted anyone there for no reason. And if they did, they were put on trial and punished for it. From handcuffs to chains, there was a variety of equipment to ensure obedience. But because there was no fear of justice or punishment out here, some people persecuted others for the sheer pleasure of it.

One day after this, Imaan met Roton Mukherjee again. When he found out what Imaan was thinking, Roton said, 'So you want to go back to jail? What you can do is, pick this stone up and go to the bus-stop. There's a policeman on duty there. Hit him on the head with it. I can guarantee you won't have to worry about food and shelter for ten years.'

'But they'll beat me up.'

Roton Mukherjee laughed. 'Nothing comes for free. If you want a place to stay, hot meals, a safe environment, you have to pay.'

'I can't do it.'

'Then there's another option. Easy. Kill yourself. Jump onto the railway lines.'

'I'll die!'

'Of course you won't die, it's all drama. Make sure there's no train nearby. And that the police see you. They'll arrest you for attempted suicide and put you in jail.'

'I didn't know such a thing was possible.'

Roton the pickpocket smiled bitterly. There are many things you know nothing about. It's not a crime to collapse on the street and starve to death. Neither for the killer, nor for the dead. But suicide is a crime.

After a pause, he looked at Imaan. 'Where's Shibpodo now?'

'I heard he's in hospital,' said Imaan.

'He's in jail, ward no. 7. The police have sent him to custody. Unlikely to be released in less than two years.' Roton sounded rueful. 'The baanchot wanted to live, and when he couldn't, he wanted to die, but he couldn't do that either. He's a cripple now. Lost both his legs below the knee. Serving time.'

Shibpodo had meant to kill himself. He had jumped in front of a train at the Loharpara level crossing, where the locals had put up a signboard saying, 'Kindly do not commit suicide here'. There was something about the atmosphere of the place that made anyone who went there in the first light of dawn feel an urge to kill themself. Some twenty people had died there this way, which was why the locals had put up the signboard. Maybe better sense would prevail on reading it, and the person would choose a different spot for suicide.

Shibpodo was illiterate, so he couldn't read the sign. His fate hadn't read it either, for in that case, he would not have had the operation.

He needed a week's rest after the surgery. He was embarrassed to limp around the hospital, so he had himself discharged and spent a few days in his own bed. When he was able to walk again, he went to meet his boss Komol Shamonto. It was afternoon, the deliveries had been made. It was time to write up the accounts. One door of the godown was closed, and the other one was ajar. Komol Shamonto was nowhere to be seen. He never left the godown, guarding the cashbox with a zeal that made Bheem say, 'Shamonto has glue in his arse, doesn't even go for a piss.' Where had he gone?

It wouldn't be right to enter the godown since no one seemed to be around. The boss had to be here somewhere, he couldn't have gone home yet, for then the doors would have been locked. But since he had been away for a week, Shibpodo had to inform him he would be back to work from tomorrow. So he waited outside the door, which opened a crack after a long time. It turned out Komol Shamonto had been inside, after all. He was drenched in sweat. When he saw Shibpodo, he said, 'What are you doing here at this hour?'

'I came to tell you I'll be back to work tomorrow.'

'Here?'

'Yes.'

'How do I take you back? You weren't here, someone had to sort the potatoes, I couldn't supply rotten stuff, after all. I hired someone else. Wouldn't it be wrong now to ask them to leave?'

Finally, Shibpodo caught sight of his replacement, who had emerged from behind the sacks. It was his beloved Aamodi boudi. She was flustered to see him here.

Shibpodo couldn't bring himself to speak. He had nothing to say, all his words had died, and so had his will to live. His long-cherished dream had crumbled to dust in an instant. He realised he would neither get his job back at Komol Shamonto's godown, nor a place in Aamodi's house, possibly not in her heart either. Komol Shamonto had swallowed him up whole like a serpent. Aamodi could realise all her dreams if she was loyal to Komol Shamonto—what could Shibpodo, a mere employee at a potato godown, give her?

Shibpodo couldn't go on this way. It would be better to jump in the path of a train. Release from all humiliation and suffering in a minute or two. And so he did. But his rage made him jump too far, with the result that the train only went over his legs, severing them below the knee. And now, life in jail was even more unbearable.

Imaan felt his heart twist at this news. His head reeled.

12

The rains had given way to autumn and then winter. The change had brought no good news, but there was nothing new in this, for it never did. But it had put Munna Mahato in danger. During the wedding season he was caught by some people he had tried to rob and beaten up within an inch of his life. He was lying on a hospital bed now, with no assurance of survival.

Times had changed, making some people rich overnight, thanks to their connections with the party or their work as land dealers or real-estate developers. Men and women from their families used the money that couldn't be put away in banks to buy flashy gold jewellery and drape themselves in it when going out.

On their way back from their social events, especially weddings, however, they took off all the jewellery for fear of being robbed on the last train, and put them in their bags. And Roton's group lay in wait to slit those bags open.

So Roton had done his ghaobaaji act on a woman's bag, taking out four bangles, a pair of earrings and a thick gold necklace, and handing them in the blink of an eye to Munna standing next to him. But Munna hadn't been able to grab them properly, dropping them to the ground. He was spotted when trying to pick them up, and was beaten up unmercifully by the people gathered around.

Munna had narrowly escaped death on the spot only because Chandona had managed to run off and get the police. 'Come quick, shepaiji, the public has captured one of us. He will die.'

The policeman was in no hurry. 'There are four of us. Take care of us first. Thousand bucks.'

Chandona shrieked, 'Save him first. I'll give you your thousand.'

'Make an advance payment,' the policeman laughed.

Chandona and the others always had some money hidden away for such situations. But she couldn't pull it out under these prying eyes. It took her some time to find a private spot where she could take it out from beneath her clothes. Luckily Munna was still alive.

The police arrested him and then told the owners, 'If you want a case against him for being caught with stolen goods, you'll have to deposit the jewellery with us. It will stay with the police till the case is resolved. You'll get it back afterwards. This will make it twenty-five per cent certain that he will be found guilty. If you want to take the jewellery back right now you can, we can't force you. But the case won't be for pickpocketing anymore, it will be for suspected theft. 379 instead of 380.'

The owners were not willing to be parted from their jewellery. They had heard from someone that gold turned to brass inside police station lockers. And so, Munna's possible sentencing changed from three years to three months. So long as he survived, he would soon be back amongst his own people.

Soon after this, a perturbed Imaan turned up at the gate of Central Jail. He had taken the bus again, forgetting his earlier humiliation by fellow passengers for supposedly being a criminal. He had considered getting off near the Kalighat temple but hadn't been able to do it.

Nonigopal Mridha was on duty at the gate. He still had his job, well beyond sixty, because his class eight certificate declared his age as being much lower. Managing unruly prisoners needed physical strength, which he lacked now. He was always out of breath after swinging his stick a few times, which was why he preferred the lighter work of gate duty. For this privilege, he had to pay a small bribe to the senior jomaadar who made the roster.

Spotting Imaan, he smiled widely and asked, 'Enjoying yourself outside?'

Imaan repeated what he had told the deputy jailer. 'Lousy place. The poor have a very hard time. Everything from food to a place to stay is difficult to get. Just that you don't have to line up and be counted five times a day, that's all.'

Nonigopal said, 'A man's life has no value outside. No one cares who lives or who dies.'

'Yes,' nodded Imaan.

'Now that you're outside, if you die, who will bury you? If you go missing who will look for you? Is there anyone?'

'No.'

'Then what are you doing outside. Come in.'

'I want to,' said Imaan, 'but how?'

'Getting out is tough, but there are a thousand ways to get in here. It's easy if you try.'

But Imaan knew it wasn't so easy. Not for him, at least. He wasn't willing to do anything that would mean being beaten up by the police. And when you were afraid of a beating, no door in the world would open up for you. Unless you knew how to give a beating and take a beating, you would never have the world beneath your feet. Imaan could do neither. Compassion and fear came in the way.

Imaan felt an urge to meet his old friends here, but for that, he should have turned up before four in the afternoon. He would also have to write a request mentioning the name, father's name, address and visitor's name and drop it in the letter box. He knew his friends' names, but not their fathers'. And he couldn't write anyway. So Imaan abandoned his plan and decided to leave. But now, he was embarrassed by his self-deception. In truth, he had come to this area not to meet his friends in jail, but to visit the cheap shacks by the creek beneath the bridge in Kalighat. There was a young woman there whom he had promised to meet again.

It was getting on for evening. The surroundings were wrapped in an unfamiliar darkness as the sun was about to set. An eerie setting. People were going home in droves, exhausted after their day's work, their lifeblood sucked out of them. Their footsteps were slow, heavy.

But those who had stepped out of their homes after resting all day looked sprightly and eager. Their pockets were lined with cash, and the city was ready with its pleasures.

There were some seekers of salvation, too, among them, who were going to the temple. And a few whose eyes glinted with lust as they kept looking into the lane on the right. But how to muster up the courage to actually enter? What if someone saw? What if the police were here? That would be the end of all honour.

Imaan was there, too, but standing on the other side of the road, unable to walk across towards the bridge and the lane beneath it. If only she were here again, if only she would take him by the hand once more and pull him along. He wouldn't offer just twenty rupees today, he would give her a lot more than anyone else. He didn't dare dream of buying her outright, but he wouldn't hesitate to pay all he had for her company for some time.

Four roads led to four different destinations. One, towards the temple, one towards the current chief minister's house, one towards Central Jail, and one towards the Hazra Road junction. Imaan followed the crowd and crossed the road.

'Ei Imaan, where do you think you're going? If it's to meet Kaalu he's still in jail.'

'No, not to meet him, I'm going to the temple.'

'Temple? What for, aren't you a Muslim?'

'When did I become a Muslim? I neither pray nor fast.'

'When did you become a Hindu then? You don't go to temples.'

'I'm not a Hindu either.'

'What are you then?'

'A human being.'

'What do you want in a Hindu temple then?'

'Nothing. Just visiting. Can't I?'

Whom was this conversation with? Had he imagined it? To hell with it all. Let everyone see, let anyone say whatever they want. I'm nobody's servant, I work hard for a living, I don't beg, I'm my own boss, I can do as I please, what business is it of anyone?

Listen, everyone. I'm Imaan. I'm here to visit Aishwarya in her house. Anything else you want to know?

Imaan went up to the tea-stall, across from which a group of young women were sitting on stools. He bought a cup of tea and stood there, his eyes on one particular door in the distance. But she was nowhere to be seen. Where was she then? Was she beneath the steps leading up to the bridge? Did the women here have their territories demarcated?

Suddenly Imaan realised a pair of eyes were probing him like searchlights. They belonged to Bibhu, who was also from the rail bosti in Jadavpur but came here to collect a supply of heroin which he peddled. He wasn't an addict himself; he only sold it to a small group of fixed customers, making enough to pay for food and shelter.

Bibhu knew Imaan slightly. He had seen him doing his rounds with his sack, but they had never actually spoken. They didn't speak this time either. Bibhu only grinned at Imaan with his yellowing teeth, conveying his thoughts. 'So you've learnt the ways of the world too. Good for you.'

He rushed off, while Imaan remained standing where he was. He didn't know how long. Eventually he told himself, why wait anymore? That lane there is open at both ends, one can walk through it. People take it to go wherever they're going. So can I, who's stopping me?

But when he stepped into the lane, he was surprised at what he saw. He wasn't carrying a loaded gun, the siren signalling a jailbreak hadn't gone off, no wild animal had broken out of the zoo—then why was everyone scurrying off? The crowded lane emptied out in minutes. Looking around, Imaan found himself standing there alone.

An innocent in the human jungle, Imaan had no idea that a police raid had begun. Which was why he kept standing like a fool instead of running away. He could easily have escaped, but he remained rooted to the spot, watching a black police van stop at the head of the lane. Plain-clothes policemen had entered already, and the entire place was under their control now. Each of them was holding a customer by his collar and bundling him into the van. A firm hand grabbed Imaan by the shoulder. 'Come on!' He was shoved inside as well.

13

It was late at night. Someone had poured buckets of tar over the earth. There was not a sound anywhere, no breeze, no current of life. Everything was in the grip of a deathly silence. Only the occasional meteor streaked across the sky.

There was a power cut in many part of the city, a transformer had gone up in flames. Repairs would not start till the morning. To Imaan, this darkness felt like the handiwork of the Devil, in the face of which even God was helpless. Closing his eyes, he tried to recollect all that had taken place since a hand at the end of a strong hairy arm had clamped itself on his shoulder. He had been thrown into the police van like a sack of paper scraps, along with fifteen or sixteen others. There was even an old man with white hair among them.

The van had stopped in front of the police station, and all of them were ushered into the office, and then, after their names and addresses had been taken down, shoved into the lock-up cells. Imaan had tripped over his father's name, simply unable to remember it. The police officer had intervened kindly and put down a former president's name, Abdul Ali. Address? Jadavpur Railway Station.

Imaan had no idea why he had been detained and what would happen now. Only later did he discover that the government had given permission to brothels with the intention of trapping customers.

From his cell, Imaan heard a desperate plea. 'Believe me, saar, I didn't do anything, I was only looking.'

'Doesn't matter,' said a police officer. 'Stepping into that lane is enough.'

'Let me off, saar.'

'Of course, we'll let you off. What are we going to do with you here? But you'll have to pay a fine. Otherwise you'll be sent to jail.'

The regulars came prepared for such eventualities, hiding in their bodies the money that might be needed for a fine. One by one they pulled out their stash and paid up. Imaan was astonished at the hiding spots. Under the soles of their shoes, pockets in their underclothes, in the fold of their collars, inside their rolled up sleeves, in their socks.

While those who had money paid for themselves, some were released with the help of friends. There were some enterprising moneylenders too. 'You don't have money? No problem, I'll pay your fine. Pay back double when you get out. Not to worry, I'll come home with you to collect. And if you don't pay up, I'll tell your family and neighbours.'

Sometimes the women from the lane turned up themselves to pay the fine, when one or more of the arrested men were their fixed customers. How would they come back tomorrow if they weren't released today? And the men would pay back the money with interest.

That was when Imaan suddenly saw the very woman for whom he had ended up in the police station. It was impenetrably dark inside the cells, with work going on under emergency lights. And in their beams he saw Aishwarya clearly, recognising her instantly, though it had been a long time. Was she here to have someone released? Whom? Could it be him? Imaan's heart began to thump. Did she see me from a distance and come running?

Imaan held his breath, feeling himself choke with gratitude. So what if we only met for a few minutes, I didn't forget you either. This was how it happened, it was all about the heart.

He jumped to his feet in excitement, only to have his illusion shattered in a moment. She wasn't here for him, she had come to get a regular customer of hers released. A constable was calling out his name. 'Which of you is Jawahar Seth? Come out, sign here and fuck off.'

Aishwarya danced off with her customer. Only five people were left in the cells now, one of them being Imaan. He was wondering whether to seize the opportunity and spend a few days in jail in the company of his friends.

Now they called for him. 'Imaan Ali, get your arse over here.' The police officer growled at him, '*Ab tera kya hoga, Kalia*? Fine or jail? Choose quickly.'

Imaan gave it one more thought. Both the doors were wide open. But his heart told him, 'It's not the right day to go to jail. I know how to get inside now, I can do it anytime. But I have to go back to that bridge, that lane. I must meet her at least once more. I must tell her that one thing I have to before I die.'

'Fine,' he said. 'How much?'

The officer held up two fingers. 'Two hundred.'

The calendar had turned over a page by the time the formalities were completed. The streets were deserted, all the shops were closed, the homeless were fast asleep on the pavements. Striding along swiftly, Imaan entered a part of the city where there was no power cut. But the lights were dim, and the darkness was still lying in ambush. A couple of mangy dogs were wandering around, a taxi passed by occasionally. Police vans were doing the rounds. A mad woman was plucking lice out of her hair. A drunk man was babbling. An expensive car stopped, its driver stepping out to piss with great confidence on the pavement.

Imaan was walking back to Jadavpur Station, since there was no other way to get there at this time of the night. The bus service would be resumed only at six in the morning. From Kalighat police station, he walked past the intersection with Rashbehari Avenue and arrived at Anwar Shah Road to his left. Here he saw a rickshaw approaching from the Jadavpur end. Bangur Hospital was nearby, perhaps a dying patient was being taken there.

But the rickshaw stopped suddenly when it came up to Imaan, and he saw Polashi seated in it. Without getting out, she said, 'They let you go?'

'Yes,' said Imaan, without thinking.

'Just like that?'

'I had to pay a fine.'

'How far up your arse did they stick the rod?'

Two hundred rupees was a lot for a ragpicker. Anyone would say it would be better to spend a week in jail. So Imaan didn't answer. He stood there, wondering how Polashi had come to know.

'What do you plan to do now?' said Polashi harshly. 'Are you going to keep standing there or get in?'

'You came for me?'

Polashi flew into a rage at this idiotic question. 'No, I came for my mother's lover. Get in!'

There was a long way to go. Imaan knew a great deal of humiliation awaited him, but he sat down next to Polashi anyway. The rickshaw set off and Polashi began her tirade. 'What the fuck were you thinking? You thought you'd go whoring on the sly and no one would find out? Now you know. You know what they say, some people are blind even when they can see. You're one of them. Fucking cow won't eat the grass outside its own door—has to have someone else's. That's you. Why did you have to run to those bitches? Will you do it again? Better not forget what happened today. I wouldn't have known if you were alive or dead. Have to thank Bibhuti for letting me know.'

Bibhu! But he had met Imaan much earlier in the evening. And this had happened later. How had Bibhu found out?

'He saw you on his way back,' Polashi continued. 'Even in the darkness he identified you, so he came to me. Polashi, the police have arrested that idiot of yours. He was whoring in Kalighat. Go pay his fine. But that's easier said than done—where's the money? I went to Bhorot, and then I was on my way when I met you. Would I have borrowed from him with interest if I'd known you had enough to pay your own fine? Would I have come running for that matter?'

'How much did you borrow?' Imaan mumbled. 'How much interest?'

Like a pressure cooker that had released steam, Polashi had calmed down a bit now. 'Five hundred,' she said. 'Maybe he'll reduce the interest if I return it first thing in the morning. Fifty or five hundred, whatever it is, you will pay. I'll get it out of you. Money doesn't grow on my father's trees.'

They had come a long way, but not a single shop was open. Imaan would have to starve if he couldn't even get a slice of bread. 'Looks like I won't get to eat tonight,' he muttered. 'All the shops are closed.'

'She didn't give you anything to eat?' Polashi hissed.

'Who?'

'You should know.'

'I didn't visit anyone. The police came even before I could.'

'Is that the truth?'

'What?'

'You didn't visit anyone?'

'Why should I lie?'

After a pause, Imaan said, 'I saw her on a bridge in Kalighat that first day I was released from jail. We spoke a little, and then I never saw her again. I went to see her today. I won't say *I* went. It was more like someone forced me to go. But before I could ...'

'... reach the shore, the boat sank,' taunted Polashi.

Both of them lapsed into silence. The wheels of the rickshaw spun across the asphalt. A fire was raging in Polashi's head. She had lost. A whore from Kalighat had defeated her. She'd have grabbed the bitch by her hair and beaten her up if she could have. It would help her to stop smouldering in rage.

Finally, they arrived at the rickshaw line outside Jadavpur Railway Station. Imaan had some money left over after paying the fine, which he used to settle the fare. It was his first time on a rickshaw—also his first ride with a young woman.

Following him on to the platform, Polashi came to an abrupt halt. 'Come,' she said.

'Where?' asked Imaan, not understanding.

'To my house. I cooked in the evening. Didn't eat when I heard about you. You haven't eaten either. We can eat together.'

Imaan was ravenous. He followed Polashi to her hut, which was about a quarter of a mile away. About ten minutes on foot along the railway line. They walked on the track, for there would be no trains now.

The shacks beside the lines were as silent as a grave. There didn't appear to be any life here. The red light of the signal was visible in the distance, shining like a one-eyed monster. The faint light oozing out of the tall lamp posts far away trickled down their faces and fell to the earth. They were walking like the only living beings in the land of ghosts. There was no moon in the sky, and the twinkling stars looked down at them in amazement.

Polashi stopped outside her door. 'Wait.' Fishing the key out from where it was hidden, she entered. 'Don't come in,

I have idols here. Stay outside.' Going in, she didn't light the lamp, but groped for a gamchha and soap. 'Come on,' she ordered Imaan.

'Where?'

'To the pond. You have to bathe,' came Polashi's stern instructions. 'You've been rummaging in filth. You have to wash it all off.'

Suddenly there was a power cut, and all the lights went out. The fear of the darkness that Imaan had felt in the police station devoured him again. They swam through the inky black night to reach the pond. Imaan stood neck-deep in the water, while Polashi scrubbed him clean.

Then, she wrapped him in the gamchha and guided him back to her shack. Entering, she located her matchbox and handed it to Imaan. 'Hold this. Let me find the lamp. Light it when I tell you.'

The matches were wet. Imaan had to scrape the matchbox several times with a match before it could be lit. In the faint, flickering flame, he saw Polashi. She was naked.

Her voice resounded in the silence. 'Look at me. Don't you dare blink, I'll blind you with my finger. Now tell me, what does she have that I haven't? Why did you have to go looking for a whore? You have to tell me. No escape for you tonight.'